PARANORMIA

PAUL REGNIER

To Dad,
Enjoy this Long Beach based journey into the supernatural.
— Paul H Regnier

OTHER BOOKS BY PAUL REGNIER

The Space Drifters series

The Emerald Enigma | BOOK ONE

The Iron Gauntlet | BOOK TWO

The Ghost Ship | BOOK THREE

PARANORMIA

Paul Regnier

Paul Regnier
PARANORMIA

© 2019 Paul Regnier

ALL RIGHTS RESERVED. This book contains material protected under International and Federal Copyright Laws and Treaties. Any unauthorized reprint or use of this material is prohibited. No part of this book may be reproduced or transmitted in any form or by any means, electronic or mechanical, including photocopying, recording, or by any information storage and retrieval system without express written permission from the author/publisher.

This is a work of fiction. Names, character, places and incidents either are the product of the author's imagination or are used fictionally, and any resemblance to actual persons, living or dead, events, or locales is entirely coincidental.

Edited by Rebecca LuElla Miller
Cover design by Seedlings Design Studio

Soli Deo Gloria

CHAPTER 1

---◆---

Greatness eluded me. It wasn't for a lack of effort or potential, as far as I could tell. I just couldn't shake the feeling I'd taken a wrong turn somewhere and couldn't find my way back.

As I lay on mold-scented linoleum, peeking through the gap under the front door of my apartment, waiting for Amber to come home, the correlation between how I spent my time and what I'd accomplished in life became all the more apparent.

"You're gonna need a tetanus shot," my roommate Steve called over his shoulder. "That floor has a pulse."

I shifted my weight, and my arm rubbed against a greasy buckle in the linoleum, as if to confirm his point. "She's worth it." The floor wasn't my favorite spot to recline, but it offered the best view of Amber's arrival, and I had to time this perfectly.

"Let it go, man." Steve spoke with little conviction. He knew I was too far gone.

Life had thrown some brutal curve balls this week. Losing my job at the movie theater and passing a kidney stone—a man's equivalent of giving birth—had constructed a sturdy wall of despair around me. People were always saying that at twenty-one life had just begun, and there was plenty of time to make things happen. This hopeful advice blew right out the window of my crummy little apartment in downtown Long Beach.

I needed something to boost my morale, and I hoped Amber would be it.

"I'm pretty sure I heard her car." I strained to hear her approach on the stairwell leading to our third-floor hallway. Either her footsteps or the bell from the elevator would signal her arrival. "She'll be here any minute."

Steve grunted. He had his back to me, nestled in his makeshift art studio wedged in the three-foot space between the living room couch and the kitchen counter. Beyond his tweed fedora that caged a smoothed, black pony tail, a dark paint brush struck mercilessly against his latest art piece. Swirling layers of thick black and grey oil on canvas grew more devoid of hope by the minute. A lone figure with an inner luminance walked through his painted darkness toward a keyhole-sized beam of light in the distance. I held little hope he would make it.

"Chris, this is stalker territory," Steve said. "She'll see right through it."

Being referred to as a stalker definitely soured the romanticized view of my plans. "Staging a run-in doesn't qualify as stalking. It just shows that I care and I'm a planner."

He finally put his paint brush down. "Just wait till you see her at Shimmer Fitness and say hello. That's what normal people do. Your plan is weird."

"My plan rules. I already waved to her on the elliptical last week. That's phase one. Phase two is when I 'accidentally' run into my hot neighbor and ask her to go to the gym. It's like a date without the pressure."

He laughed. "And you wonder why you're single. It's supposed to rain. No one wants to go to the gym in the rain, especially late at night. Abort mission."

"You suck. I need this. You know that."

Steve's art stool gave a metallic squeak as he spun to face me. His eyes were serious behind prescription Ray-Bans. Whenever he got that sober expression, he resembled an Asian version of Johnny Depp.

"Who keeps trying to get you out of this apartment?" He motioned to the low-lit, pea green wallpaper of our prison. "Who told you to submit your comic book to a publisher?"

"Graphic novel."

"Whatever, man. It's good stuff. What are you waiting for?"

"I already sent out submissions. They got rejected."

"Twenty rejections is nothing."

"Twenty-four."

Steve adjusted his glasses, his jaw clenching. "Everyone gets rejected at first. If it's your dream you gotta keep going. Or just do it yourself. Do that self-publishing package you told me about."

"It's eighteen hundred dollars," I said. "I'm broke."

"Okay, fine. Future goals. Meanwhile, you gotta get out of this apartment. You should come with me to Bible study this week. You haven't been there in months."

"Maybe they can lay hands on my wallet."

Steve pursed his lips. "You know, my cousin Miyu was there last time. A woman who actually wants to talk to you. No stalking required. She said you remind her of Daniel Radcliffe."

I sat up. "Really? Harry Potter?"

He nodded. "So now that your kidney stone is gone and you've spent plenty of time home with your video game recovery program, what's your excuse?"

"I'm busy."

"You're unemployed."

"I'm busy thinking."

"Come on man, don't neglect the spiritual. Showing up is half the battle."

I sighed. "Well, maybe God could show up a little more and inspire me."

Steve put his hands up. "Thin ice, man."

"Sorry. Long week. I need something on a Biblical level to turn things around. If there was ever a time for divine intervention, it's now."

Steve took a squeaky turn back to his brooding art piece. "Careful what you wish for."

The elevator bell dinged. I laid back down, and my eyes narrowed toward the space under the door. Thin shadows broke the light at the far end of the hall. Someone was coming. I sprang to my feet and made sure my ear buds were tucked in tight and straightened my black Adidas-branded T-shirt. I checked my phone. Ten-thirty. Was it too late? Was my fake run-in idea desperate and transparent?

I turned to Steve for a confidence boost. "How do I look?"

Without a glance he shook his head, his shiny black pony tail giving a lazy swoosh. "Sad. This whole idea is just sad."

"Sad like that depressing painting?" I pointed to the maelstrom of darkness dominating his canvas.

"That's cold-blooded, bro."

I opened the door and strode into the hallway with an energetic pace. I kept my eyes on the ground, bobbing my head to imaginary music from my earbuds. I took a quick glance between head-bobs. Someone was coming closer. Definitely her. She headed for her door, which was across the hallway, mere steps from mine. Destiny.

My timing was perfect. After a few steps toward her, I looked up, as if I'd been consumed with my music and was surprised to find someone else in the hallway. "Oh, hey Amber."

She was in her waitress uniform, but her shirt was untucked, and an apron hung over her shoulder. Her soft brown hair with caramel streaks was disheveled, and her brown eyes held the glassy haze of a busy weekend dinner crowd. But even still, her beauty ignited my nerves. Having her so close threatened to overthrow my cool demeanor and unmask the desperate loser within.

Several Chinese food take-out boxes weighted a to-go bag hanging from her hand like an anchor. She was headed for a late night snack.

"Hey." She gave a tight-lipped smile and flicked her eyes toward her door. Uh-oh. Red flag. She was tired and hungry, and I was a distraction. A speed bump and not an oasis. No, I was looking into it too much. Maybe she just had a tough day.

I tried a friendly smile. "Long night?" *Long night?* That's the best I got? It was practically an insult.

"Yeah." Her eyes flicked toward her door again. I was dying fast.

"Well, I'm off to the gym." For some reason I put my hands on my hips. Was I a superhero? "Sometimes you gotta go late to keep the momentum going." The nerves were kicking into overdrive, and my lips took on a life of their own. I didn't even know what I was saying anymore.

"Mm-hmm." She gave the smallest nod I'd ever seen in my life. "Well, I'd better get going." She grabbed keys out of her purse with the agility of a ninja. Suddenly her door was open, and she was moving inside. The window of opportunity was closing fast. I hadn't laid on nasty linoleum for five minutes so things could end like this.

"Hey," I heard myself stutter, "if you ever want gym motivation, just hit me up." I jerked a thumb back at my apartment door as if she didn't know where I lived. "Not that you need it, but, you know, easier to stay motivated with someone, you know, helping motivate you." I was a crazy person at this point. How many times had I just said the word *motivate*?

"Oh, okay. Maybe." She moved deep into her apartment like she was gaining distance from a grizzly. "Enjoy your workout. Bye." The door closed tight almost before the word *bye* shot from her lips.

More than one security lock clicked into place. Terrific, my dream girl was afraid of me. Steve was right, I'd stumbled into stalker territory. If only I could take back the last few horrible moments of my life. My one consolation was that no one else was around to watch the train wreck.

A creaky hinge signaled the door to my apartment opening wider. Steve was standing in the doorway, holding his black, swirling canvas. His eyes bounced slowly from the closed door of Amber's apartment to me.

He pointed to his artwork. "And you call *this* depressing?"

My face of defeat must have prompted mercy. He set the painting back in the room, grabbed a ring full of keys, locked up, and headed toward me.

"Come on," He slapped my shoulder as he walked by. "Let's hit the gym."

Basking in the cranked heater settings of Steve's lowered economy car while storm clouds loomed overhead was another painful reminder of my poor decision to buy a motorcycle. One cursed summer day I caught my now ex-girlfriend eyeing a guy with superhero biceps and tats on a motorcycle. My ill-fated jealousy went home that day and spent all the money from my shoebox labeled, *car fund*. Needless to say, the motorcycle didn't keep my girl and pushed hopes of a car further into the future than a crystal ball could see.

Despite the gas money saved, the close calls I'd been in from cars swerving into my lane and the suffocating wrap of thick leather gear I had to wear to avoid skin grafts, had driven the allure of riding a motorcycle straight out of my head. Plus, I didn't have the biceps or tats to draw the attention I was after in the first place.

At this point, I was even jealous of Steve's ten-year-old, oxidation-infested beater.

It was no surprise that plenty of gym parking spaces were available on a stormy Friday night. A flash of lightning lit up the clouds as we headed from the car to Shimmer Fitness. It felt like a warning.

The gym was wedged between a storm drainage channel and a busy street. The channel, or "wash" as we called it, was a concrete monstrosity that made natural rivers seem sleek and elegant in comparison. A dark river of nasty runoff rushed along in the storm channel. Apparently it was already raining close by.

Low rumbles of thunder sounded right before we ducked into the gym. Safe and sound. Now that we were inside, the thumping house music was all that remained. It drove us forward on the treadmill like the kettle drum of a slave ship.

Shimmer Fitness at eleven on a Friday night isn't what you see in the glossy promotional material. The intense, corporate types had already tracked their progress with electronic wristbands and headed home to dream of yachts. The slick hipster crew were off exchanging ironic observations between shots at some trendy Irish-style pub, and late night teenagers were avoiding creepy slackers like me who chose to work out in the dead of night.

"Perfect time to be here." Steve had a zen-like smile as he walked the treadmill.

"You're crazy," I said. "It's a ghost town."

Besides us, only a few stragglers haunted the spongy black floor of Shimmer Fitness. The late night, tattoo-laden gym crowd were mostly restaurant and club workers looking to add some agility and muscle before heading back out with the other vampires.

"It's peaceful," Steve said. "You can really focus on your workout."

"Yeah, what are you burning, like two calories an hour?" I said. "It's not a forest path. You're supposed to run."

He continued walking, unfazed. "Hey man, I'm only here for support. I don't need to lose weight."

Steve was right about that. He'd had the same trim appearance since fourth grade. Lucky metabolism for someone who sat around painting all day.

"Maybe not, but you should hit the weights," I said. "Wouldn't hurt to put some meat on them bones."

"I have kung fu skills. I don't need brag meat."

I laughed. "Just because you're Chinese doesn't mean you know kung fu."

"That's racist."

"No, what *you* said was racist."

"Whatever, racist." He smiled and brought the treadmill up to a jog.

The late night, motley crew of gym rats strained against the dead machines around me. A taught, yellow banner dominated the far wall trumpeting the gym's slogan, "Achieve Greatness."

Just reading it made me feel small. A hollow sensation swirled in my gut. "You ever feel like you went down the wrong road?"

Steve raised his eyebrows. "Should I stop this thing? This sounds serious. You wanna talk it out?" He pointed to the exit. "Taco Bell?"

"No, man. I don't want to get into a big thing. I just ... Didn't you think at this point you'd be doing something better? Meaningful. Y'know, something great?"

"I am. My art is great."

"Come on. No offense, I think it's cool, but you've only sold, like four paintings. If it wasn't for your generous grandma, you'd be living on the street."

Steve frowned. "My grandma is my investor, just like any new business has. And the money only comes in if I maintain a 4.0. You sure you want to talk money Mr. Unemployed?"

I put up my hands. "Sorry. You're right. Look, you know I like your art. It's awesome. But it's not like, changing the world or anything."

"Says who? I've found my place. Change happens when you find your sweet spot and dig in."

I huffed out a laugh. "How can you be all yoga master when we live in a tiny apartment that smells like old cheese in downtown Long Beach. That's not greatness."

Steve shrugged. "Greatness is relative."

In roommate discussions there was always a point where things fell silent. Steve was either on a higher spiritual plane or in denial. I wished I could be that content.

After a few minutes we hit the panting stage that happens to people whose gym attendance is spotty. We spoke only when necessary using few words.

"Five more minutes?" Steve looked over, fumbled a bit on his footing, and recovered, keeping his focus dead ahead from that point forward.

I shook my head. "I gotta stop. That kidney stone messed me up." The kidney stone excuse was pure nonsense, but the intense pain it put me through a few days ago was worth at least one exercise dodge. I hit the stop button and felt the wonderful sensation of the roller slowing down under my Nikes. I checked the digital readout: 12 minutes. 94 calories. Not bad.

Steve was already off the machine, wiping his face with a towel. "Let's beat it. This place is dead."

"I thought you said it was peaceful."

"Changed my mind."

We trudged toward the semi-circle welcome desk like we'd just run a marathon. Rain spatters decorated the wall of windows at the exit.

Steve pointed outside. "Rain. Told you."

"Hey guys. How was your workout?" A tight, blue shirt could barely contain the Captain America clone headed our way from the welcome desk. His golden name tag looked like it was going to spring off his over pumped pecs at any moment. He had his clipboard ready and was sliding the pen out like a sword from it's sheath, ready to slay us. "There's a few spots left for our summer training. I can set you up with a full nutrition plan for half price. This week only."

He stood in front of the exit like a bouncer guarding a private club. His eyes slid from me to Steve, his pen poised against his steel clipboard of doom. He was waiting for one of us to cave.

"No thanks, man." I retrieved earbuds from my pocket and plugged my ear holes, thwarting his attack. "We're good."

"No doubt." Captain America smiled and nodded as if we'd just conquered villains together. "You guys are hitting it late at night. You're way ahead of the game. You're good, that's for sure. Question is, do you want to be great?"

I froze as if he'd hit me with a spell. "Yeah." The words escaped my lips before I knew what was happening.

Captain America grinned and pointed at me with his pen. I was about to get knighted. "Excellent. What's your name?"

"Chris Loury." What was I doing? Why didn't I throw out a fake name? I could've said Harry Potter and been safe from his records.

His pen etched my name in clipboard stone. There was no way out now.

"I'll look you up on the member list." He lowered the clipboard and held it tight to his side like a shield. "I'll call you. We'll set up a program." He headed back to his watchtower. "You fellas have a great night."

The light rain and frigid air outside the gym instantly turned my warm sweat marks into ice water.

"What the heck was that?" Steve hugged at his chest to keep warm. "Personal training?"

The wind spat the rain right into my eyes. Everything was conspiring against me. "Yeah, like I'm gonna call that meathead back."

"Bad move, man," Steve said. "He'll be after you every time you walk in. It's because he said the word, 'great,' isn't it?"

"Well, what's wrong with wanting to be great? That college pastor you want me to go back and listen to always talks about doing great things."

"Yeah, for other people."

"Well, maybe God should give me better directions. Is it too much to ask for some clear signs?" I looked up into the falling rain. "God, help me out here. Open my eyes. What do you want me to do?"

A loud peal of thunder sounded overhead.

Steve gave a wary look at the sky. "Thor's coming. Let's get out of here."

We jogged to his silver clunker, and he scrambled for the keys. A single beep sounded, and Steve opened his door.

I tried my handle, but it wouldn't budge. "Hey, you only unlocked your door."

He rummaged around in the back. "I know, I'm getting a towel."

"Come on, it's freezing. Open up."

"Just a sec. You're all wet. You'll ruin my seats."

There was another peal of thunder followed by an unmistakable cry for help. I squinted through the rain and spied a dark figure hanging over the edge of the storm channel. He was less than thirty yards away.

"Hey!" The man lifted his arm up as if to signal me, losing a few inches of ground in the process. "Help!"

"Oh no." I felt paralyzed. What was I supposed to do?

Did cops handle this? Firemen? "Steve! Call the cops. Or an ambulance or whatever."

Steve lifted his head from the car, shielding it with a fast food bag. "What?"

The rain was coming down harder now, and thunder rumbled, making it difficult to hear.

"Call the cops. That guy's in trouble."

Steve scanned the parking lot. "What guy?"

"Just call 'em. He's falling into the channel."

"Okay." He ducked back into the car. I saw the blue glow from his cell phone through the window.

Without thinking I bolted toward the channel. What was I doing? I could barely hang for twelve minutes on a treadmill, and I was rushing to rescue someone?

The clouds lit up like God just took a picture of my ridiculous actions to laugh at later. A loud boom echoed through the parking lot. I remembered hearing something about the time between the flash and the sound of thunder signifying the proximity of the lightning strike. Whatever the exact calculation was, it was close. Too close.

"Hurry!" The man was losing his grip on the top edge of the channel. All I could see was his head and grasping arms. If I didn't do something quick, he would slide right into the river of filth.

I sprang onto a sagging metal fence, the only barrier between me and the wash. The wet fence bowed as I scrambled over it, the rough cross pegs on top scratching my arm like claws. I flung myself to the other side of the fence, falling to my knees on cement.

The man reached toward me, his eyes wide. "I'm slipping!"

I hurried forward. The wind was strong, threatening to send me over the side along with my intended rescue. I crouched and grabbed the metal base of a no trespassing sign to keep from falling in.

Leaning forward, I held out my free hand. "Grab my hand!"

He paused, looking afraid to try. Now that I was close, I could tell he was a young guy, probably around my age. A neon green T-shirt with parachute pants pegged at his ankles screamed midwest thrift store. Had to be a tourist.

The brown river of run-off surged beneath him.

"Come on." I called out. "I'll save you."

His green eyes seemed unusually bright as they connected with mine. The flashing skies were probably playing tricks on me. The hint of a smile ran across his lips.

He reached for me. His fingers were just inches away. I leaned forward, stretching as far as possible without losing my grip on the sign post. His fingers brushed against mine. A thrill of hope went through me. This was going to work. I was actually going to save this guy.

The sky flashed a blinding white, and lightning struck the metal sign post I clung to. Every muscle in my body locked up. My body arched in pain as fire shot through my bones. A scream escaped from my throat, sounding foreign to my ears.

CHAPTER 2

I awoke to the calming hum of a car engine. An old Police song softly poured from the speakers.

My head rested against the window of the passenger seat. Outside, dull yellow street lights shone on the rain slicked sidewalk speeding by. Distant points of light drew my gaze further out to oil refineries squatted like floating ghost towns in the night ocean. Recognition flickered in my mind. I was headed down the Long Beach coastline on Ocean street.

New car smell hung in the air. I adjusted my position in the seat creating a moist, squishing sound. My clothes were drenched. Wait, how did I get in a car? Who was driving?

My head jerked over to find a young man with black hair behind the wheel of a BMW.

"Morning, sleepyhead." He smiled and tousled my wet hair.

"Hey." I batted away his hand and backed as far from him as the car door allowed. "Who are you?"

"Aw, you don't remember me?" He rubbed at his cheek as if wiping away a tear. "The guy whose life you tried to save?"

My memory flashed to his wide-eyed face reaching toward me as he slid into the wash. Only, now his hair was dry and styled, and he wore a sharp, black suit. If it was daytime. I'd imagine he was a young exec racing to a power meeting with other ladder climbers.

"Oh. Right," I said. "Guess I passed out."

"Lightning will do that to you. I'd say you're lucky to be alive, but statistically speaking, ninety percent of people struck by lightning survive." His green eyes were unnaturally bright, almost luminous. My guess was some kind of enhanced contacts.

I looked down to find a ring of water soaking into his fine leather upholstery. "Uh-oh. Sorry, man. I'm all wet."

He waved a dismissive hand. "Don't worry, it's a rental." He laughed as if indulging in some private joke.

"Oh no." I pulled a dripping cell phone from my pocket. "My phone."

"No worries." He grabbed the phone from my hand and blew into it as if extinguishing a birthday candle. He handed it back. "Good as new."

I grabbed it. "Very funny."

My phone lit up bright, all the app icons sliding into place. "Whoa. That's weird."

"My pleasure. That thing is tiny. New model?"

"Not really." My phone read 11:40 p.m. The street lights ticked by. Where were we headed? Why was I in this guy's car, and what happened to Steve? A feeling of apprehension spread over me.

I tried to talk casually as if my guard didn't just go up. "Thanks for pulling me from the wash." I slipped a hand into my wet gym shorts pocket. My fingers wound around my keys, holding them ready in case I needed a makeshift weapon. After all, I had no idea who this guy was. Long Beach was a mixed bag. "Where are we, anyway?" Even though I knew exactly where we were, I wanted to get him talking so I could have time to plan an escape.

"You never drive down the coast?" He raised an eyebrow. "You live at 7235 Hemlin Street, only four-and-three-quarter miles away, and never visit the ocean? That's a travesty."

I narrowed my eyes and pressed my shoulder against the passenger door. "How do you know where I live?"

He pointed to my pocket. "Your license. You were passed out for a while so I looked through your things."

The creep factor was ratcheting up with this guy. It was time to bolt. Ocean Street curved inland, heading for Second Street. Lots of late night spots were still open. This would be a good place to escape. I just had to wait for the right moment.

"Well," he said. "We've got a lot of work to do. Plenty of chances for greatness." He looked at me. "That's what you wanted, right?"

I gave him a studied look. "You listening in on me? Did you overhear me at the gym or something?"

"Nah, it's all there in your file." He leaned over, opened the glove box, and pointed at an overstuffed binder.

I kept a careful watch on him as I retrieved the binder. The first page was enough to give me chills. It read like a spy dossier with me as the subject. Not only did it have the typical records you could find online, but there were summaries of my life history and personal experiences. I flipped the page and landed on a paragraph that explained in great detail how I stole a pack of Juicy Fruit gum when I was seven—something I never told anyone. I slammed the binder shut and threw it like a hot coal back in the glove box.

"Who are you?" My heart was flying. I tried my best not to sound panicked. "You with the government?"

He chuckled. "Hardly. I'm an angel. You've been granted a supernatural experience."

My mind was spinning too fast. My mouth opened, but nothing came out.

He smiled and nodded. "I know. It's a lot to take in. Problem is, we don't have a lot of time. A supernatural experience is a visible event in the spiritual world. Chances are, we'll have company soon. Bad company. Things could get messy."

"Look, this is a mistake. Whatever this is, I don't want to get involved."

"Well, it's a little late for that. You're the one that sent the request up, aren't you?"

"No. You got the wrong guy."

Crazy, green-eyed angel guy frowned and pointed to the windshield. A visual appeared on the glass like some futuristic car with an embedded movie screen. I gasped at the realization that it was me on the visual. I was in my apartment talking to Steve.

"Let's just take a listen, shall we?" He turned up the volume on his car radio, and the conversation I had with Steve earlier that night swelled through the speakers.

"Well, maybe God could show up a little more and inspire me."

Steve put up his hands. "Thin ice, man."

"Sorry. Long week. I need something on a Biblical level to turn things around. If there was ever a time for divine intervention, it's now."

The visual switched to Steve and me walking outside the gym as it started to rain. I was talking to Steve with animated gestures.

"Well, what's wrong with wanting to be great?" I was saying. *"That college pastor you want me to go back and listen to always talks about doing great things."*

"Yeah, for other people."

"Well, maybe God should give me better directions. Is it too much

to ask for some clear signs?" I looked up into the falling rain. *"God, help me out here. Open my eyes. What do you want me to do?"*

The visual went dark. Suddenly my mouth was really dry.

"See?" Angel guy pointed at me. "All you. Not my fault. I'm just a messenger. The good news is, now your eyes are opened and chances at greatness are right around the corner. Sound good?"

Things were getting out of hand. This was some serious voodoo. Maybe I was drugged, and this was a bizarre hallucination. I had to get out of here and clear my head.

"Listen man, it's late. I gotta get home." I wondered how bad it would hurt to jump out of a moving car.

"Mm." He shook his head. "Not a good idea. You'll miss your first mission."

In a flash I pulled out my keys and wrapped the key ring around my knuckle. I gripped tight and aimed the keys his direction. "Stop this car and let me out. Now!"

He glanced at the keys, amused. "Don't get all weird. You have work to do."

"I said pull over!"

"Listen, you can't—" An old-style telephone ring sounded between our seats.

He grabbed a chunky white phone docked by the stick shift. It was nearly the size of a brick.

"Yeah?" He spoke into his brick phone. "Oh, come on. I didn't ask for this. He's a DH6, you can't expect ... But ... Fine." He clicked off the phone and clunked it back on the dock. "Now look what you did." He frowned and pulled the car to a stop in the bike lane.

I yanked at the door handle, but the door was locked.

He stared at me with his bright green eyes. "I'm warning you, this is a bad idea. You're vulnerable. One foot in the natural, one in the supernatural. It's not safe out there."

I swiped the keys through the air as if they were a knife. "Open it!"

He grunted. "Figures."

There was a click, and I yanked open the door, falling to the curb in the process. The door slammed shut, and the BMW sped away. I focused on the back of the car to get a license plate. Unfortunately they were new frames with a logo instead of plates. The only personalization was a red bumper sticker on the back that read, "Ask Me About Free Will."

I scrambled down an embankment of wet ivy that led to rows of houses. A light drizzle was all that remained of the earlier downpour. I fumbled for my phone while taking cover in an alleyway and dialed Steve's number. After a few rings it went straight to voice mail.

"Come on," I hung up. "Where are you?"

The Uber app icon lit up on my phone and started flashing. I'd never seen it do that before, but they were adding new features all the time. I hit the app and a message read, "An Uber driver is near your location. Need a ride?" A "YES" button flashed below.

"Perfect." I tapped the button.

Headlights swung into the alley heading straight for me. I backed away as a silver DeLorean skidded to a stop. The signature gull-wing door rose up.

A young guy with a mop of bleach-blonde hair and shades leaned over from the driver's seat. "You the dude that needs a ride?"

"Yep. That was fast. I'm a little wet, is that okay?"

He grabbed a Baja hoodie from the back and threw it on the passenger seat. "Not a problem."

I jumped inside and closed the door. "Thanks. Cool car."

"Yeah, it's gnarly." The DeLorean lurched forward, heading into the street. "Where to, brah?"

"Um..." My mind was still scrambled. I had to get home. "...Can you take me to 7235 Hemlin Street?"

He put a fist in the air. "Righteous."

I leaned back and let out a long breath. "This night is one for the books."

He nodded. "Yeah? Totally bogus, huh?"

This guy was straight out of an 80s surfer flick.

"Yep. I just need to get home."

"Oh, you know what, bro?" Surfer Boy said.

"What?"

"You should totally do that rad mission first."

I tensed. "What'd you say?"

"Man, you know..." He turned to look at me, lowering his glasses. Luminous green eyes sparkled. I froze. It was BMW guy. "...The mission."

CHAPTER 3

How in the world had this psycho tracked me down? And where did he get this car and a wardrobe change so fast? Bad mojo was coming down with the rain, and I had to get out of here.

I yanked out my keys again, jabbing the air between us. "You freak. Who are you?"

"What'd you think?" His voice switched back to normal. "Did I nail that character or what?"

I yanked at the door handle. It wouldn't budge. "Unlock the door. Now!" I jabbed toward him with the keys.

He narrowed his eyes. "Enough with the keys. We're wasting time."

"Pull over!"

He sighed and slowed the car, pulling toward the curb. "Freewill is a generous gift, you know. It shouldn't be abused."

I yanked at the door handle. "Let me out!"

"Okay, but like I said, bad things can happen out there without my guidance. You should really rethink this."

"Open!"

He threw up his hands. "I told them you wouldn't listen. Typical DH6."

The handle clicked open, and I jumped out. I bolted down the neighborhood street in the opposite direction. Second Street was dead ahead. The lights from the storefronts held the promise of people. Safety.

I rounded the corner and ended up in front of a bank. Headlights cast blurry reflections on the street as the sparse traffic cruised by. A few late night revelers still walked, or stumbled, down the sidewalk. A guy with an oversized army jacket and a grizzly beard sat hunkered near the bank ATM. He played Bob Dylan on a beat-up guitar, a few crumpled dollars resting in a guitar case at his feet.

My phone rang. To my surprise, I still gripped it in my hand. Stress did weird things to your perception skills. An image of Steve filled the screen.

"Steve!" I practically screamed in the phone. "Man, am I glad it's you."

"Where are you? I'm freaking out over here." Steve's typical low key speech pattern had vanished. It sounded like he was hyperventilating. "I told the cops you were missing. Is this one of your stupid jokes?"

"What? No. This night has turned insane. I got hit by lightning. Some guy saved me from falling in the channel, but he's a lunatic. Says he's an angel and keeps talking about a mission. Oh, and he's some kind of quick change artist, or he has a twin or something and–."

"All right, I'm hanging up."

"No! Dude, I'm serious."

"Stop messing with me." The worry in Steve's voice changed to annoyance. "I spent an hour in that parking lot looking for you. In the rain! I thought you fell in the wash. Is this a joke? You're recording this for YouTube, aren't you?"

"Listen to me, I swear as your best friend, I'm in trouble. I need your help."

There was a long pause. "You swear?"

"Yes. On my life."

He sighed. "If you're messing with me, I'm never helping you again."

"I'm not, I promise. Can you pick me up?"

"Where?"

Several bars and clubs were still lit up. A tropical themed dive called The Spinning Parrot was half a block away.

"I'll be at The Spinning Parrot on Second Street."

"Okay ... This better not be a trick." The line beeped off.

For a moment I thought about calling the cops, but how on earth would I explain all this? Right now, I just wanted to be around people and get out of the cold air.

I headed for the club and just as I hit the crosswalk, something dark moved past the corner of my eye. When I stopped to look, there was nothing but shadows on the wall of the club. I wanted to dismiss it as a trick of the eye, but something was off. The shadows had moved. On their own. I searched the darkness for a moment hoping to find a hidden black cat or scavenging rodents to explain things.

Suddenly, there was a squeal of tires, and I spun to find bright headlights bearing down on me. I sprang from the crosswalk to the curb as a grey El Camino roared by.

My heart was pounding as if it wanted to leap out of my throat. Something between a cackle and a cough sounded next to me. I turned to find a homeless man leaning against the traffic light. He was wearing an olive green jumpsuit that appeared to have recently been through a mud run. He mowed down on a cheeseburger as he delighted in my near death experience.

"Almost gotcha." He pointed at me and cackled through several missing teeth. "Watch yer step, boy." He took a sloppy bite that dribbled Ketchup into his scraggly beard and continued staring as if waiting for more entertainment with his meal.

Walking the streets around midnight was filled with teachable moments. I gave the cheeseburger hobo a tight lipped smile and headed into the club.

The hazy, eleventh hour crowd at The Spinning Parrot was having it's last hurrah. It was less than an hour till closing time, but the house music was still blaring. The guys hunkered at the bar were slurring out tales of past glory while the bartenders were busy wiping down the counter and glancing at the clock. A group of middle-aged women in matching yellow dresses formed a circle on the dance floor. They danced arm in arm like they were at a Greek wedding. I felt like I was walking in late on a movie.

Even though it was only drizzling outside, my clothes were long past the light sprinkle stage and heading toward drenched-vagrant status. I kept to the shadowy paths of the club hoping the bartenders wouldn't notice my soggy condition and kick me out. A passing waitress gave me a double take like she knew something was off. I tried to act casual and as soon as she looked away, I slid around a fake palm tree to avoid her scrutiny. Unfortunately, someone was already standing there.

I collided with a blonde woman in a white cocktail dress, and she crumpled to the floor.

"Sorry." I bent down to see if I'd hurt her. "Are you okay?"

The face that turned to me was the face of an angel. Her vibrant blue eyes winced from the collision. "Yeah, I think so."

I offered my hand. "Here."

She took my hand, and I helped her up. I froze for a moment, not used to seeing her level of beauty outside of a movie screen. With her flowing blonde hair and form-fitting white dress, it was as if she just stepped off the volleyball court of a beer commercial and went for a night on the town. An intoxicating floral scent wafted toward me.

"Sorry," I managed. "I wasn't looking. I'm just ... Sorry." Just once, when it really counted, I wish I could've been smooth.

"It's okay." She looked me up and down. "Why are you all wet?"

"Oh." I looked down as if I just realized it. "Yeah. Long story."

She raised her eyebrows and let out a small laugh. "Okay." Her eyes locked onto something behind me. "Here comes trouble."

Headed toward me was a giant. My mind wavered on whether he reminded me of a garbage truck or a pit bull. I prepared a list of apologies in case this hulk was her boyfriend.

"Do me a favor?" the woman said.

"Huh? Me?"

"Just pretend like we're together." She moved next to me, hooking my arm with hers as if to assure my beating.

The hulk reached us and was obviously ready to smash me. His narrowed eyes ping-ponged between us. "Who's this guy?"

"This is my boyfriend," she said.

It was like hearing my death sentence pronounced in a courtroom.

"Um..." My head was spinning. I couldn't manage anything else.

"Oh." The hulk's shoulders slouched. His expression switched from intense to confused. "Thought you were alone."

She gave him a playful punch on his wall of arm. "No, silly."

"But—"

"Listen,"—she grabbed his monster hand—"can you grab me a lemon drop martini? When you get back, we'll talk about it."

His eyes slid from her to me as if he was shifting the targeting site on a rifle. "Boyfriend, huh? This guy?"

She put her hand on my chest. "Yes. But I always like to meet new people." She smiled at him. "Why don't you get me that drink, and we'll talk about it."

He gave her a sly grin. "Sure." He gave me a glare for good measure, then turned and lumbered toward the bar.

She waited a beat, then pulled me forward. "I need to dodge that guy," she whispered. "Walk with me?"

"Okay." Better to leave with the hottie than get pummeled by the giant.

In a matter of seconds we were out the front door and back into the cool night mist. She held my arm tighter in the cold, which I didn't mind in the least, and headed down the street.

She giggled. "Just because he's an MMA fighter he thinks he can get any girl he wants."

Suddenly I felt very breakable. "MMA? Serious?"

She waved a dismissive hand. "Don't worry, we're free. You saved me." She winked. "Thank you ... Um ..."

"Chris."

"Thanks, Chris." She smiled. The moonlight gleamed off the gloss of her pouty lips. I was in love. "I'm Solas."

"Wow. Cool name." Why? Why couldn't I be smooth?

The sound of a door clicking open came from behind us. I peeked over my shoulder. The MMA hulk walked out of the club, scanning the street.

"Uh-oh," I said.

"Hurry." Solas sped our pace to a fast walk, her heels clicking on the sidewalk the way a spooked horse might sound. She retrieved her keys from a glossy white purse the size of a hamster. I couldn't imagine much more than a lipstick and cell phone fitting in there.

A car alarm chirped and the headlights of a gold Porsche 911 flashed at the curbside before us.

"Come on." Solas let go my arm and waved me toward the car as she trotted street side.

"Whoa. This is your Porsche?"

She laughed as she opened the driver's side door. "It was a gift."

"Hey!" The hulk spotted me. He jogged down the sidewalk headed my way.

"He's dumb, but he's dangerous," Solas said. "We should go."

I nodded and scrambled into the Porsche. It was like getting into a luxury spaceship. The engine purred to life. With a chirp of the tires we launched from the curb, then coasted through the rain-slicked street as if we were floating.

"Say 'bye to the ogre." She glanced toward The Spinning Parrot and gave a theatrical wave.

The hulk watched us leave from the sidewalk. He studied me as we passed as though saving the memory of my face for his bucket hit-list.

"Oh, man." I cast a mournful look at the fine leather underneath my wet gym shorts. Chalk up two luxury car seats ruined in one night. "Sorry about the seat. Do you have a towel or something?"

"Oh, don't worry. James will fix that."

"James? Your boyfriend?"

She laughed. "No, I'm single. James is the parking manager at The Silver Towers. I pay him extra to take care of things."

"Silver Towers? Nice. I heard they have an Olympic sized pool on the roof."

"And a hot tub. But it looks like you already went swimming tonight."

"Yeah, sorry. It's been a wild night. I tried to save this guy who was falling into the storm channel."

"Is he okay?"

I nodded. I didn't know how to explain the weirdness about old Emerald Eyes, so I just left it at that.

"That makes two people you saved tonight." She flashed me a warm smile. "You a superhero or something?"

I was pretty sure this was God telling me to marry this woman. "Nah. Just a weird night."

"Well, thanks again. Listen, can I ask you a big favor?" She put her hand on mine.

"Uh, sure."

"That guy knows where I live. At least the building. Would you mind walking me to the door. I hate to ask since you've already—"

"Yeah, of course." I tried a confident nod as if to bolster my non-existent body-guarding abilities.

She squeezed my hand and smiled. "I knew there were some nice guys left in this city."

As bad as the night started out, it was improving by the second. Of course, if the hulk came after us, I was little more than a speed bump in his way. On the other hand, if he didn't show up, I'd come out of this a hero with the possibility of a date.

I stared in awe at the futuristic dash for a minute. "This is probably the greatest car I've ever ridden in."

"Thanks."

"You in movies or something?"

"Let's just say I have connections in Hollywood."

"Nice. Good work if you can get it, right?"

"Yep. What line of work are you in?"

Uh-oh. Any chance I had with this future starlet was about to come crashing down.

I decided to play it vague. "Um, I'm an artist."

"Really? I know a local art dealer. There's an exhibit this weekend. Maybe I can get you a spot."

"No, not that kind. More like, illustrations. Storyboards."

"Like comic books?"

So much for keeping my nerd-hood secret. "Sort of. Graphic novels."

"I love those."

I turned to her, making sure this moment was actually happening. "Really?"

"Oh, yeah. Forces beyond mere mortals battling it out. It's riveting."

Was it too early to propose? "Well, maybe I can show you some of my work sometime."

"I'd like that."

The traffic light turned green as we hit Bay Shore Avenue. Solas turned left like we were part of a movie car chase. The back end swung out toward a parked car, then slid away just in time as she corrected the steering.

"Whoa. That was crazy," I said.

She chuckled. "Fun, huh?"

A muffled ringtone came from her mini purse. She retrieved a gold Bluetooth earpiece from the dash and put it on. "Yes? Mm-hm." She grinned.

A line of yachts sped by my window as we drove along the marina. Driving in a Porsche passing rows of yachts was definitely not my typical Friday night.

"I see ... No problem." She took off the earpiece and grabbed my hand. "Will you do me a quick favor?"

"Sure."

Solas pulled the car over to the curb. "You see that boat right there." She pointed to the largest yacht docked near us.

"The big one with the blue stripe?"

"Mm-hmm." She leaned over, opening the glove box. Inside was a red present with a golden bow. "Drop that by the back door."

I stared at the present for a moment. "Christmas coming early this year?"

She smirked. "It's a thank you for an old friend of mine. It has to be tonight. I'd do it, but I'm in heels and that dock sways. Please?" She hit me with both puppy-dog barrels of her blue eyes.

"All right, I guess." I grabbed the present. "You sure it's cool?"

"Don't worry, it's fine. Unexpected gifts work wonders for keeping powerful connections happy."

I stared at the shiny red gift for a moment. This night couldn't get much weirder. "Okay. Be right back."

"Thanks, Chris. The gate code is 5343."

I got out and headed for the gate to the marina. The late night mist against my wet clothes was like walking through spider webs made of ice. Now that I was out of the sweet car without that angelic face beside me, delivering a present to a yacht at midnight felt a bit insane. I glanced back at the gold Porsche. Solas waved and blew me a kiss. She was definitely out of my league, but maybe she was tired of dating the wealthy and gigantic. Maybe I was the down to earth guy she'd been waiting for. Maybe I was delusional.

I reached the black iron gate to the marina and entered 5-3-4-3 into the keypad. The door clicked open, and I was on my way to the dock. The marina was empty. Besides my footsteps on the wooden planks, the only noise was the calm lapping of sea water against the pristine white hulls of the boats. I took a deep breath that seemed like opening a fridge where someone kept expired fish.

My cellphone rang, making my heart jump. It was amazing how loud it seemed when everything else was calm. I checked the phone. Steve. A surge of guilt went through me.

I clicked on the phone. "Steve! Dude, I'm so sorry, I—"

"Save it man." His voice was calm and disconnected. "I'm at The Spinning Parrot and you're not here. I knew you were messing with me."

"No, no, I had to get out of there. This big guy was gonna kill me, but I left with this smoking hot chick in a Porsche who actually likes graphic novels. Can you believe it? Anyway, I'm over by a bunch of yachts right now and—"

The phone beeped off.

"Steve?" I called into a dead phone.

I redialed, but it went straight to voicemail. "Steve, listen, I'm not messing with you. This has been the craziest night of my life. I'll explain everything but right now I'm with a major hottie. See you soon." Hopefully he wasn't too mad, and I could smooth things over later.

Now that I was on the docks, the yachts towered over me, sending a visual reminder with my every step that even though they were boats, they were bigger and nicer than my apartment. A ramp led from the dock to my goal—a massive yacht with a thick, blue stripe.

I headed across the ramp and dropped onto the back of the boat. There was a door flanked by windows, leading into the interior of yacht heaven. I could imagine cushy, ocean themed decor just inside.

As I started forward, a light clicked on in one of the windows. I froze. For some reason I assumed no one would be on board. A shadow moved across the light inside. A wave of panic went through me. What was I supposed to do if they opened the door and found me? What if they thought I was a thief, and they had a harpoon gun handy?

The shadow grew larger, headed straight for the door.

CHAPTER 4

My adrenaline spiked as the shadow moved toward the door of the yacht. Why did I ever agree to drop off a gift on some random stranger's boat? Powerful people owned yachts. People with lawyers. People that would take one look at my guilty face and wet gym-rat clothes and zap me with their gold-plated taser gun.

"Screw this." I tossed the present by the door and raced back across the platform.

A door banged open behind me. I broke into a sprint and headed for the gate. Thankfully, the gate opened from the inside without the code, saving me an awkward pause. Soon I was back at the Porsche, fumbling to get the door open.

I jumped inside and slammed the door behind me.

She chuckled. "What's wrong?"

"Someone was on the boat." I gave her a serious look. "Why didn't you tell me?"

"Aw." She pinched my cheek. "You're cute when you're paranoid."

I looked back toward the marina. A flashlight was sweeping the dock near the boat I just came from.

"See." I pointed to the flashlight. "They're looking for me."

"Relax." She revved the engine and peeled out, launching us back onto the street. "You just did a good deed. If you're worried, I'll call the mayor tomorrow. Tell him it was me."

"The mayor?" My eyes went wide. "What if he thinks I was breaking into his yacht? He could send the whole police force after me."

"Boy, are you wound up tight." She shook her head. "I told you, I have friends in high places. It'll all work out."

I stayed quiet for the next few blocks imagining all the ways a powerful mayor could ruin my life. Maybe she was right and I was being paranoid. After all, I didn't do anything wrong. Hopefully, this experience was just another stupid thing I would laugh at later.

The Silver Towers Luxury Apartments loomed just ahead, like a glistening cylinder from an alien world that landed in the midst of the squat cardboard boxes of normal buildings. Solas headed for a descending ramp that lead to underground parking.

The Porsche sped through the concrete parking structure, between rows of parked cars, silent and unmoving, like prostrate servants as their king passed. Solas maneuvered the car into a reserved spot near an elevator.

"We're here." She shut off the car and got out.

I joined her outside, taking in the grey structure around us. For some reason I'd imagined walking her to an outside entrance. Now that we were tucked away right next to the elevator, walking her to the door for protection seemed unnecessary. But hey, if it made her feel safe and gave us more time together, who was I to argue?

"Nice parking space," I said.

"Come on." She motioned to the elevator. "I'll call you a cab upstairs."

Upstairs? Was she asking me up to her room or just to the front desk? My nerves started kicking in big time. I followed her inside the elevator, pretending I was taking it all in stride.

The elevator was covered in polished steel with subtle depictions of palm trees, waves, and seagulls. Solas inserted a key next to the lit button for floor twenty. The penthouse. We weren't stopping at the front desk, we were headed straight to her swanky room. What on earth had I said or done for this supermodel to take me up to her room? Was she actually into me? Maybe she was just being nice and calling a cab.

"Penthouse, huh?" My voice cracked.

"Mm-hm. Wait till you see the view."

Steve would definitely have to forgive me once I told him this story.

She glanced at my drenched Adidas shirt. "I have some dry clothes you can borrow."

Borrowing clothes meant returning them. Another chance to see her. "Sure."

A soft ding sounded, and the elevator doors opened to Xanadu. The inside of her apartment could have swallowed mine three times over. A curving wall of windows granted an elevated view of Belmont Shore and the nearby marina. The dark streets and buildings were stitched together with lights that seemed to glow in the mist.

Her heels clicked against white marble floors as she stepped inside. Most of her furniture was either cushioned white fabric or finely crafted, polished glass. Golden throw pillows graced overstuffed white chairs and couches. It was as if a high-priced designer fashioned a cloud into a luxury suite.

She dropped her keys with a sharp clank on a glass entry table and spun around. "Home. What do you think?"

Obviously, the place was spectacular. I shrugged. "Eh. It's okay."

Solas grinned and narrowed her eyes, sauntering over to me. "You little devil." She drew close and pointed at my chest. "I'm going to have to watch you, aren't I?"

"Me? I'm an angel."

Solas gave an impish smirk and ran her finger down my cheek. "I knew I was going to have fun with you."

She was actually enjoying our back and forth.

"C'mere." Solas turned and led me to a hall closet. "This should fit you." She pulled out a black suit along with a white button up shirt and black tie.

"A suit?"

"You prefer your wet clothes?"

"No but, I ... Suits aren't really my thing."

She held it up to me, looking me up and down. "I bet you'd look great in this."

I saw an Armani tag. "Armani? What if I mess it up?"

"Don't worry about it. And you can put your wet clothes in this." She handed me a plastic bag and pointed to a bathroom. "Get dressed."

I held up my hands. "Your home. Your rules." I grabbed the suit.

Soon I was out of my wet clothes and suited up, though I was having a little trouble trying to remember how to knot a tie. The bathroom, of course, was all shiny chrome and spotless white surfaces. My mind was spinning through the variables of what I was supposed to do next. Should I make a move? Was I reading too much into this? What would a cool guy do in my situation?

A knock sounded at the bathroom door. The tie was crumpled around my neck like a defective noose. I opened the door, and Solas was standing there drumming her fingers against her hip.

"Having trouble?" she said.

"This tie is broken."

She smiled and went to work on the tie. Within seconds it was fastened with a neat knot. She smoothed the tie down across my chest and took a step back.

"Not bad." She nodded.

"I feel like I should be holding a martini."

"Great idea." She winked. "Rain check. Your taxi's out front."

"Oh." Well, that answered my question. She was just being nice. "Thanks."

"Go through the lobby." She grabbed an envelope from a pristine white kitchen counter and handed it to me. "And can you give this to the concierge on your way out?"

I grabbed the envelope. "Your caviar and champagne order?"

"You're cute." She pinched my cheek. "Just say it's from Ms. Callow."

"Aha. Now I have your full name. I can stalk you on social media."

Solas grinned and sauntered away. My eyes followed with tractor-beam precision until she reached the bedroom door and paused, looking back at me. "Until next time, Chris." She blew me a kiss and disappeared behind the doorway.

I shook myself back to reality and headed for the elevator.

In the lobby, a thin man with a well-trimmed goatee was speed-typing at the front desk.

With my slick suit on, I waltzed up like I belonged there. "You the concierge?"

He folded his hands and gave a tight smile. "Yes. Can I help you?"

I handed over the envelope. "This is from Ms. Callow."

He was quiet for a moment, his eyes glancing around the room as if looking for errant dirt smudges in the otherwise pristine lobby. He grabbed the envelope and slid it into his coat pocket. "Thank you. And you are?"

"Bond." I straightened my tie. "James Bond."

The concierge scowled as I turned and headed back into the cold night.

A taxi was idling right outside. The driver was a bearded guy with dreads. His head was waving back and forth like a drunk metronome as Bob Marley flowed from the speakers.

I jumped in the back, a musky wave of incense like a stagnant cloud, waiting for me. "7235 Hemlin Street."

The driver gave a slow nod. "Not a problem, mon."

The taxi pulled into the street like a whale moving through syrup. Obviously, this guy lived life on his own schedule of mellowness. I checked my phone. 12:45 and no call back from Steve. Time to work on my apology speech.

"Hey, mon." The driver called back. "You be thinkin' of doing that Irie mission yet?"

My eyes snapped up. "You gotta be kidding me!"

He turned back, his bright eyes green as summer clover. "No, mon. It's high time for the mission."

CHAPTER 5

My heart raced. I checked the door. Locked. "Who are you? Stop following me and let me out, you freak!"

"Relax. I come in peace, mon."

"Drop the voice. You're a lame stereotype."

"Really?" He frowned, his voice switching back to normal. "This was my best character. I was actually saving it for later, but you keep running away so I have to burn through all my favorites."

I dialed 9-1-1 on my phone. "I'm calling the cops."

He snapped his fingers. My phone went dead. I tried to power it back up, but the screen stayed black. A hollow sensation spread through me. This was no ordinary street lunatic. He had to use some serious electronic wizardry to kill cell phones. Did I accidentally piss off the wrong government official?

"Now," Green Eyes said, "before you stab at me with your keys again, let me explain. You're my assignment."

I paused a moment. "Is this a government thing?"

He chuckled. "No. I told you, I'm an angel."

He was sticking with the angel story. Maybe I was caught on one of those hidden camera shows. People would be laughing at my panic. Reveling in my paranoia. Whatever was going on, I decided the best way to escape was to play along. After all, he already had my address. I just needed to make it home, lock the doors, and call the cops.

I relaxed into the seat and took deep breaths to ease my stress. "Angel, huh? Where's your wings?"

"Invisible," he whispered. He wiggled his fingers in the air and made a spooky ghost sound.

"You're kind of a punk for an angel."

He let go the steering wheel and turned to face me. "Really? I thought I was being impish and delightful."

I pointed to the street. "Hey! Look out!"

He waved off my concern. "All under control."

The steering wheel took on a life of it's own, navigating through the street with precision.

"Neat trick," I said. "Listen, um ... Gabriel, is it?"

He looked skyward. "I wish. Name's Finchelus. When I'm on assignment, I usually go by Sir Edmund Finchelus." He held out his hand.

I gave his hand a tentative shake. "You British?"

"I'm whatever I want to be." His voice took on a British accent.

"Whatever. Listen, why don't you just tell me about this mission thing, and I promise I'll get right on it. That way you can float back up through the clouds, and we'll both be happy."

He huffed out a laugh. "If only. Even Mother Teresa needed more prompting. You're a DH6. I'll be stuck down here for a while just to make sure you get it right."

"DH6?"

"Difficult Human, level 6."

I frowned. "That sounds pretty judgy. I thought God saw me through eyes of love."

"He does. But, as you know, His ways are higher than ours. We angels need classifications. Definitions for ease of communication within the heavenly realms. Nothing personal."

"Yeah, well, it sucks. Angels are supposed to be kind and helpful."

He spread his hands out. "This is why I haven't been on assignment since 1985."

Tonight was definitely going down as the weirdest night of my life.

"Well, time's a wasting." He turned back around and gripped the steering wheel. "Let's get to your mission."

The last thing I wanted to do was get out in the cold, misty air again. Especially to do whatever his demented sense of a mission was.

Up ahead was a bank with a lit up ATM in the parking lot. A brunette woman walked toward it. As we neared, I did a doubletake when I recognized Amber, my next door neighbor. A tall guy with a wild shock of brown hair and wrap-around sunglasses was shadowing her.

"Wait," I said. "Pull over."

"But what about—"

"Pull over! Someone's in trouble."

The cab slowed and pulled to the curb. Amber was almost to the ATM. The guy following her had his hands stuffed deep in camouflage jacket pockets. He was grooving as if listening to music even though he had no ear buds.

A nervous energy surged through me. "That guy is trouble. Call the cops."

"He hasn't done anything," he said.

I glared at him. "Count to ten. Then call."

He nodded toward the woman. "If you're so sure, maybe you should do something."

"What about you? You're an angel, right? Use your holy power."

He shook his head. "Not my jurisdiction."

My muscles tensed. What was I supposed to do? What if he had a gun?

"Listen," I said, "do you have a weapon handy? Can you snap your fingers and get me a taser or something?"

"Against regulation."

The man was only steps away from her.

"Thanks for nothing." I got out of the car and headed into the parking lot. I sure hoped she knew Kung-fu because my one semester of Judo wasn't coming to the rescue.

Late Night Sunglasses grabbed Amber by the wrist and spun her around. She screamed and struggled against his grasp, kicking at his shins.

"Hey!" I rushed toward them. My heart was beating like a speed bag.

Sunglasses looked back at me, without losing his grip on Amber, then pulled a knife with his free hand.

I skidded to a stop right in front of them.

"Back off suit." Sunglasses pointed the knife toward me.

I froze, my eyes locked on the blade. Motion out of the corner of my eye broke my focus on the weapon. A big guy with a wife beater and a shaved head emerged from the shadows of the parking lot.

"Man, where you been?" Sunglasses hissed at him.

Wife Beater had to be six foot two or better. As he closed, the tattoos covering his arms and neck came into focus. His body was an artistic canvas of death. Cobras slithered through skull eye sockets, hollow faces were frozen in agony, and dragon fire left fields of skeletons forever lifeless on his forearms. The inked army of undead was outlined in vibrant red as though it was about to return from the grave in order to hurt me.

"Who's this guy?" Wife Beater jerked a thumb at me.

Sunglasses shrugged. "Some suit with bad timing."

Wife Beater turned on me. "Beat it, Suit."

It was so foreign to my ears to be called 'Suit' that I paused a moment. I glanced at Amber. Her eyes were wide with fear.

In my panic, I said the first thing that came to mind. "Let her go." What was I doing? I almost sounded as if I was daring him to stab me.

Wife Beater tightened his fists and his mouth turned into a thin line. He was about to bring the pain.

All my muscles tensed. My mind spun through desperate options of what I should do next. For some reason, my brain stalled on the question of why anyone would go outside in this cold wearing just a wife beater.

Amber reached into her purse, pulled out a small bottle, and in one motion sprayed something into Sunglasses face. He howled in pain.

Wife Beater lunged toward me, pushing me back with both hands. I fell back, feeling as though I'd just been back-kicked by a mule. I hit the sidewalk, my head smacking against concrete. My vision blurred. For a second I thought I was going to pass out, then everything stabilized.

I sat up and took in a terrible scene. Wife Beater struggled with Amber, trying to take her purse. Sunglasses staggered like a drunkard nearby, wiping his face on his sleeves and cursing.

In my graphic novels, I put superhero characters in situations like this all the time without a thought. Now that it was me, it was far more terrifying.

As if the situation wasn't already bad enough, my eyes were playing tricks on me. I saw what looked like heat waves from the desert flowing up from the shoulder blades of the thugs. Combined with the heat waves were streams of black smoke as if their clothes had been on fire. I must've hit my head pretty hard.

Whatever happened next, I knew I couldn't just sit by and see Amber get hurt. I scrambled to my feet and raced toward them. Having already felt the wrath of Wife Beater, I went for the smaller, injured target. I barreled into Sunglasses and sent him into the brick wall of the bank. There was a muffled cry as he smacked into the wall and crumpled to the ground.

I stumbled, almost tripping over his fallen body. My feet found solid footing, and I looked up just in time to see Wife Beater's fist close in on my face.

CHAPTER 6

Everything was a swirling kaleidoscope of objects. Amber, the ATM, the brick wall, the night sky—all blurred together in a twist of colors. Voices spoke nearby, their sound distorted as if traveling down a long, metal pipe.

My vision adjusted, a few remaining black spots dissipating like the corrupted section of an old film. I was somewhere between sitting and lying down, propped up against the wall of the bank. A trail of lipsticks, Tic Tacs, and pens littered the pavement nearby. Amber kneeled before me, gently slapping my cheek.

"Chris?" She slapped a few more times. It stung.

"I'm okay." I grabbed her hand to prevent more slaps. I glanced around the area. Our attackers were nowhere in sight. "What happened?"

She sighed and sat back. "I was robbed."

I leaned forward. "Did they hurt you?"

"I'm fine. I got some good scratch marks down the big guys arm."

I imagined his creepy tattoos bleeding. "How much did they steal?"

Her face tightened as if she was holding back tears. "Well, aside from my license and credit cards, about eight hundred in cash."

"Eight hundred! It's one in the morning. Why are you here with that much?"

She squinted at me, and her lips tightened. Her moment of sadness was quickly heading toward another fist in my face.

"Sorry." I tried to diffuse the moment. "None of my business."

Amber looked down, defeated. "No, you're right. I was trying to avoid a bounced check. Plus, I didn't like the thought of that much money in my apartment."

I nodded. Now that I was fully awake, the sensation of throbbing pain on my left cheekbone screamed for attention. "Is there a mark on my cheek?"

She winced like it was painful to look at. "It's pretty red. And swollen. You'll probably have a nice bruise."

The spot was tender to the slightest touch. "Fantastic."

"It's weird that you're here." Her brows knitted. "I mean, I'm really glad you showed up, but, you know, it's ironic."

"No kidding. I was driving by and saw that guy following you. I had my taxi drop me off just when things turned ugly."

She looked at the street. "What taxi?"

I followed her gaze. My green eyed Rastafarian angel and his taxi were no where in sight. Figured. He hounded me all night, then, when I really needed him, he vanished. "Terrific. He took off."

Police lights flashed as a black and white pulled up to the bank. A siren chirped on and off like a gym teacher's whistle calling class to attention. Two cops got out and headed toward us.

"I called them while you were out," Amber said. "Maybe they can track those guys down."

Soon we were recounting the story of the late night ATM thuggery to the police.

Amber filled in the gaps of the story after Wife Beater knocked me down for the count. Apparently she'd used her purse as a makeshift nunchuck, getting a few solid hits in before the contents exploded onto the ground. She mentioned how the sunglass-wearing thug was bleeding from his head and dizzy because of his trip into the wall. I, of course, took this as a personal victory. Somewhere between dizzy Sunglasses and Amber's purse pummeling, the thugs decided we were too much trouble. They grabbed her wallet from the strewn contents of her purse and took off.

The cops took dutiful notes, all our personal info, and promised to look into things as they headed back to their car.

Amber gave a compassionate look at the sight of my swollen cheek. "Need a lift?"

"Sure."

Amber drove a nineties olive green coupe. I felt as if I was riding in a large cough drop. Still, smaller interior meant I sat closer to her, which was a bonus.

Street lights ticked by, glowing in the mist like distant moons.

The ride was quiet for a little too long, so I figured I'd break the ice. "Sorry about earlier tonight. The whole workout invite thing. I was in kind of a weird mood."

"That's okay." She gave a quick, forced smile. Obviously she still thought I had been a bumbling moron earlier at her apartment door.

"Yeah, I dunno. I guess I just wanted to get to know you better. There's probably a hundred less awkward ways I could have tried."

"Well, getting punched in the face protecting me was

pretty good." She leaned over and pulled down the sun visor. Thin lights lit up around an embedded mirror. I leaned forward and checked my face. A deep red mark ran along my swollen cheekbone.

"There goes my modeling gig tomorrow," I said.

She laughed. A little too hard.

"By the way..." She glanced over at my Armani. "What's with the suit? You moonlighting at a piano bar or something?"

I chuckled. "Nah. I got drenched earlier. A friend let me borrow this." It felt strange calling Solas "a friend," but I didn't know how else to refer to her.

"It's a good look for you," Amber said. "I'm used to seeing you in a T-shirt and shorts."

Women liked guys in suits the same way guys liked women in cocktail dresses. Even though we'd all rather be wearing sweats, somehow we preferred seeing each other dressed to the nines in uncomfortable clothes.

"Thanks," I said. "So, do you always go to ATMs at one in the morning?"

She narrowed her eyes in a playful manner like she was about to punch me. "It was twelve forty-five. I was trying to cover bills from Caring Tables. They were already late. I didn't want to bounce their checks too. I was gonna go earlier, but the restaurant was a zoo tonight and I forgot."

"Caring Tables? The homeless place, right?"

"Yeah. It's a soup kitchen."

"You work there?"

"Volunteer. It was supposed to be a summer thing. I'm going to culinary school, and I thought it would look good on my resume. But once I started, I kind of fell in love with the place. Plus, half the staff left when the semester started. They didn't have enough people, so I couldn't just leave. I took this semester off to help."

Beauty and a heart. What a woman. "Wow. Modern day Mother Teresa."

She rolled her eyes. "Hardly. So far I've broken their oven, busted one of the bathroom pipes, and put a big gash in the front door. And now, I lose the money to cover their bills." She shook her head. "Maybe I should've just gone back to school."

"No, you're doing a good thing." I tried to reassure her. "We should all be doing stuff like that."

She flashed a grin at me. "You really think so?"

"Absolutely. I know I should volunteer more."

"Well, we could definitely use your help at Caring Tables. Are you free this week at all?"

Uh-oh. Check mate. How did I walk into a volunteering gig so blindly? "Um, yeah, I'm not really a good cook. I'd probably just make a mess of things."

"Oh, we need all kinds of help. Handyman tasks, food serving, clean up. No special skills required."

Being that my handyman skills consisted of installing a new toilet paper dispenser in our apartment that broke off two weeks later, I pictured myself sweating over giant kettles of smelly stew or on my knees scrubbing a toilet used by the homeless. What a grim future. Still, it would assure more face time with Amber. Plus, with my new volunteer-guy persona, she'd no longer look at me as the weird gym guy next door. I might actually have a shot at a date.

"Okay," I said. "I'm not sure how much I can help, but I'll do my best."

The corner of her mouth turned up, revealing a cute little dimple. "Trust me, any help is appreciated."

All too soon we were back at our building. In the last few minutes of our drive, her dimples and brown eyes had tricked me into volunteering at Caring Tables tomorrow for lunch. I said goodnight and headed for my apartment.

It felt good to be back home, cramped and smelly hole that it was, after such a bizarre night. I closed the front door and slumped against it, the fatigue of the craziness catching up with me.

Steve was still up working on his swirling painting of despair. He didn't even turn at my arrival. Silent treatment.

"I get it, you're pissed," I said. "I'm sorry, but I wasn't messing with you. Everything I said was true."

"Which part?" Steve continued his painting, not bothering to turn around. "Yachting with supermodels or getting struck by lightning?"

"Can you just give me a chance to explain?"

"You disappeared in the gym parking lot. You told me some guy was in trouble and to call the cops. By the time I finished the call, you were gone. I got drenched searching the parking lot for you. I checked the storm channel. You weren't there."

"I was. I tried to save this crazy guy, but then the lightning hit me. I blacked out. He must've dragged me to his car. I woke up in the dude's BMW."

Steve let out a long breath and set his paintbrush down. He finally turned to face me, his eyebrow raising in the process. "What's with the suit? And what happened to your face?"

I shook my head. "Where do I start. This night is beyond anything ever. I'm going through some serious paranormia, and I need you to trust me with what I'm about to tell you."

"Paranormia?"

"Yeah. You know, like a supernatural experience that completely freaks you out."

"I don't think that's a thing."

"Whatever, can I tell you what happened?"

He leaned back with a sigh and motioned for me to continue.

I launched into the full story of lightning, the emerald-eyed angel, the Porsche-driving hottie, and the thug attack on Amber at the ATM. Steve listened with patience, but his scrunched up face spoke volumes of skepticism.

After I finished, he scratched his head, letting out a stifled laugh in the process. "I don't know, man. You sure you aren't exaggerating a little?"

"Dude, I swear it all happened," I said.

"Don't take this the wrong way, but I took two semesters of psychology. Sometimes the brain can tweak a little when life gets thin. Your imagination adds some excitement back in your experience, you know?"

"You think I'm imagining all this?"

"No, just amping it up a little."

"You can ask Amber about the ATM. It happened. We filed a police report. Everything I told you, happened."

He frowned. "Then why aren't you burned? You got hit by lightning, right?"

I looked down as though I might find a fresh burn mark. "I don't know. Just lucky, I guess."

Steve nodded slowly. "And this guy that says he's an angel. He dresses like characters from the eighties?"

I held up my hands. "Man, I know it sounds ridiculous. Maybe he's one of those TV magicians. He probably had cameras rolling the whole time."

"Uh-huh. And Amber, the same girl who brushed you off tonight, is suddenly interested in you?"

"Yeah. I mean, maybe. She smiled at me a lot. Smiles with dimples. That's a sign, right?"

Steve pursed his lips. "And this blonde supermodel, she was into you, too?"

"Yes. I think. This is her suit." I motioned to the Armani.

He tilted his head. "She wears suits?"

"No. I don't know, she just had it."

Steve stood and trudged toward his room.

"Wait," I said. "You gotta believe me."

He sighed. "Look man, I get it. Life is tough right now, but whatever all this is with the hot chicks and angels and everything isn't gonna help." He walked through the doorway of his bedroom, then turned again. "It's late. You should crash. It'll do you good."

I nodded, and Steve headed off to bed. When I thought about it, I really couldn't blame him. My story sounded insane. The problem was, it all happened.

The excitement of the night was catching up with me. Just hearing Steve say *crash* made my eyelids heavy, but there was one thing left to do before sunrise.

I made a quick call to the police to report the green-eyed stalker. It didn't go as well as I planned. After describing the costume changes my new angel friend went through, the tone of the call shifted and suddenly they were asking if I'd had anything to drink or taken medication.

After a half-hearted assurance that they'd send a patrol car by my apartment to—as they put it—"check on things," I hung up, and as soon as my head hit the pillow, I was out.

CHAPTER 7

I woke up bleary-eyed and checked the clock. The red digital readout said, 11:14. I was living on vampire hours. Soup time started at twelve-thirty at Caring Tables. Another chance to see Amber. I'd be in her element. She'd be all relaxed and more open to laughing at my jokes and falling in love with a fellow volunteer. At least, that was my hope.

I got up and checked my face in the mirror. A deep red mark on my cheekbone was heading toward purple. I suppose it was better than a full black eye.

A few, unsure moments ticked by as I peered into my dresser, deciding between the Iron Man or the Green Lantern T-shirt. Which one would get more heckled by the homeless? My mind drifted back to the cheeseburger hobo laughing at me after the El Camino almost ran over me. I pictured him in the soup line, pointing and laughing as ketchup dribbled down his beard.

I grabbed the Iron Man shirt, imagining it would shield me

from ridicule, and headed for the kitchen, hoping there was enough milk left for cereal.

Steve had scrawled a note and mounted it under a fridge magnet.

Chris,

I'm meeting a nuclear-physicist-swimsuit-model for breakfast, and then I'm off to MIT to split the atom with my bare hands. See you tonight.

- Steve
P.S. We're out of milk.

I frowned, spying a freshly emptied milk carton in the trash. What a punk.

Half way through a day-old donut and orange juice fortified with calcium, my phone rang. It was a local number I didn't recognize. "Hello?"

A woman's voice came over the line. "Good morning, Chris." Her tone was silky and familiar. "I'm meeting one of my clients for lunch. He's an executive in the graphic novel industry. I told him I knew an aspiring artist, and he wanted to see your work. I thought you might like to join us."

"Solas?"

"Miss me?"

"Yeah. How'd you get my number?"

"You were easy enough to track down. Listen, why don't you bring some of your graphic novel work and meet us at Magaris Steakhouse. Say, twelve-thirty?"

"Really? Yeah, okay. Oh, wait..." My promise to Amber came rushing back. Lunch at Caring Tables was at the same time. "...Um, I'm supposed to do this thing . . ."

"Can't you reschedule?" Solas said. "I don't meet with this

client very often. This could be the start of something big. Just explain how important this is to you. I'm sure they'll understand."

For a moment I was speechless. How could I possibly pass this up? Amber wouldn't expect me to put volunteering over my career. Besides, I could always make it up to her. I'd volunteer for two days instead of one. "Yeah. Sure. I'll be there. Thanks, this is really great of you."

"My pleasure," she said.

"Should I dress up or something?"

"No," she said. "Be yourself."

"Okay, great."

"See you soon." She clicked off.

I felt ecstatic and guilty at the same time.

A few minutes later I was in the hallway knocking on Amber's door. She opened it and leaned against the frame clad in a white T-shirt, jeans, and cowboy boots. The only thing she lacked was a Stetson, and she'd be a cowboy's dream. I suddenly wished I was a cowboy.

Amber glanced at my shirt. "Hey Iron Man. You ready?"

How could I cancel on this woman? I decided to dodge the question instead. "You wear cowboy boots to a soup kitchen? Aren't those expensive?"

"Eh, I wear these everywhere." She lifted a boot as if kicking a tumbleweed. "Reminds me of home."

"Texas?"

"Los Angeles."

I paused for a moment, not understanding the connection. She laughed. "I'm just messing with you. I didn't grow up around cowboys. I just like wearing them."

Beautiful, caring, and playful. She was really ticking off the checklist of my ultimate girl.

"I'm heading over there early." She came into the hallway, closing the door behind her. "You want to go with me?"

Man, how I wished I could say yes at that moment. "So, here's the thing, I just got this crazy opportunity that could really turn things around for me."

"Oh." Her playful spirit was noticeably muted. "I understand."

"I promise I'm not trying to get out of volunteering. I really want to help, but I've been desperate to get my artwork seen and finally there's someone—"

Amber held up her hand. "It's okay, Chris. I just had another volunteer cancel. It happens. I'd better get going though. We'll be a little short staffed." She turned to leave.

"Maybe I could come by later," I tried. "I mean, there's always more homeless to feed, right?" The second the words were out of my mouth I regretted it. The off-handed comment didn't come out at all like I planned. What I meant to be a helpful offer sounded more like an insult.

Her face tensed. "Sure, Chris. Sounds good."

I could tell she thought I'd never show up at that kitchen. I had to fix this.

"I'll come in this week," I said. "All week for lunch. I'll be there." What had I just done? In my rush to make things right, I overshot. I'd just promised away my whole week.

She searched my eyes for a moment as though trying to understand where I was coming from. Good luck with that. Even I didn't know.

"All week?" she said.

"You bet," I said with some weird, spur of the moment, manufactured assurance. "I'll be there at twelve-thirty all week. I'll even swing by today after my lunch meeting is over." If I kept going like this, pretty soon I'd be donating a kidney.

Amber nodded, her eyes brightening a bit. "That's really great of you, Chris. I hope I'm not making you feel pressured or obligated or anything."

Obligated, no. Incredibly motivated by her hotness, yes.

"What?" I gave her a dismissive wave. "Of course not. I want to do this."

    She smiled. "That's awesome. I'll be glad to see you there."

    "Yeah, me too."

    Amber headed down the hallway, glancing back for a moment. "Good luck at your meeting."

    "Thanks."

    Meeting. I had to get my graphic novel together, fast.

The Long Beach sun was out in full force. It was late September, and the great ball of fire in the sky wasn't ready to let summer go quietly. The wind tearing against me felt great as I weaved my motorcycle through traffic, but I knew the moment I stopped, my protective leather gear would bring on the sweat.

    I pulled up to Magaris Italian Steakhouse at 12:22. My typical five to ten minutes late habit didn't overthrow my plans this time, and I was actually early.

    Magaris was like an authentic Italian joint reimagined by yuppies. The food was supposed to be great but way too expensive for my feeble wallet.

    My motorcycle nestled into a narrow spot right up front. Great parking was one of the fringe benefits that helped counter the dangers of riding a bike. That and the cool leather jackets I wore for safety. I hoped the jacket combined with my messenger bag slung over one shoulder projected a rugged, Indiana Jones vibe.

    As I set the bike on it's kick stand and pulled off my helmet, quick movement caught my eye. A cluster of shadows gathered under a sycamore tree in the parking lot. I could've sworn a husky dog or something of similar size had just darted under it. I examined the shadows for solid shapes but found none. Even though I was under the angry September sun, a chill swept over my skin.

I studied the shade under the tree a moment longer. A group of shadows was darker than it should have been. My phone rang and I jumped, my heart skipping a beat. I didn't recognize the number, but it was a local call.

"Hello?" I said.

"Good morning. Or should I say afternoon? You're a late sleeper." It was the green-eyed angel. As much as my brain wanted to deny the fact that he had my number and the nightmare from last night continued, his voice was unmistakable. It had all the excitement and sharpness of a teenager wrapped in a richer, melodious blues/rock singer quality.

"Finch?" I said.

"The name is Finchelus. I'm glad you're well rested because we've got missions pending."

"Look, I don't know what all this is about, but I'm not interested. When I'm around you, bad things happen. I almost got stabbed last night."

"My report said mild abrasions," Finch said. "When you mess with the supernatural, there's always an element of risk, everybody knows that."

"No, they don't. I don't. Listen, I don't know what your game is, but I'm out. Leave me alone." I hung up the phone.

I checked the shadows beneath the tree one more time. All seemed normal again. I shook my head and started toward the restaurant.

My phone rang. I checked and sure enough, it was Finch again. I sent it to voicemail and continued forward. The text alert sounded. I sighed and checked the text.

> Was it something I said?

I switched the ringer to vibrate and headed for the entrance.

As I strode toward the front door, helmet in hand, I saw Solas. She was seated by herself in the patio area next to a three tier, garden fountain carved from white stone. A few thin rays of sunshine broke through the foliage-covered lattice overhead. They illuminated her long, golden hair and sparkled off the fountain water behind her. The scene seemed as though it moved in slow motion.

Not watching where I was going, I tripped over a step. When I recovered, her eyes were locked on me, beckoning me over to the table.

After convincing myself she hadn't seen my stumble, I strode up to the patio table, trying to look confident.

"Hey, you." She stood revealing a gold summer dress with a hypnotic array of sparkles.

"Hey." For some reason I waved with my helmet hand. It was like making some bizarre toast to bikers. I hoped it didn't look as weird as it felt.

She met me as I reached the table and gave a warm embrace. Her body felt incredible against me. I didn't want to let go.

"Glad you're here." Solas pulled away, her attention locking on my cheek. "Ouch. What happened?"

"Oh, I got jumped at an ATM last night." I said it in a nonchalant way as if the experience was normal for a street-wise guy like me.

She paused a moment. "Really?"

"Yeah. Someone was in trouble. I had to step in." I was pushing the limits of my hero facade.

Solas placed her hand on my shoulder. "You have a whole career ahead of you. No need to play the hero. You need to take care of yourself."

I nodded. "Yeah, I know."

She motioned to the table. "Have a seat."

I joined her at the table and set my jacket on the chair, enjoying the cool breeze moving through the shaded patio. Two glasses of champagne were already waiting for us.

Solas lifted her glass. "To your future as a professional graphic novelist."

"I'll drink to that." I clinked my glass with hers and took a long drink. "So, who's this graphic novel guy that's meeting us? What company does he work for?"

"John Mullen. He runs his own management service. Represents a lot of artists like yourself."

"Great. Hey, thanks for inviting me. This is huge. If there's anything I can do for you, just let me know."

She studied me a moment. "Well, I am in need of an assistant."

I paused, not knowing how to respond. "Oh. Really?"

"Yes," she said. "Nothing complicated, just daily errands. It's good money. Something so you can pay the bills until your graphic novel takes off."

My phone vibrated. I clenched my teeth. "One sec." I checked the text.

> Hey again. Finchelus here. Are you ignoring me? By the way, I'm trying to get up to speed on your current technology and speech. How's this?
> BRB, TTYL, LOL. :) :o ;\
> Does that mean anything to you? I can't say I fully understand the purpose.

This time I shut the phone off before tucking it in my pocket. "You were saying?"

A waiter in a maroon shirt and black vest arrived. "Ready to order?"

"Tuscan style filet mignon, medium rare with grilled asparagus and steak fries." She looked at me. "Should I make it two?"

I smiled. "I wish. It's a little pricey. Maybe just the fries."

"Don't worry, I'll take care of it." She winked and handed our menus to the waiter. "Make it two orders."

"Coming right up." The waiter hustled away.

"Wow, thanks." I couldn't remember the last time I had expensive steak. My mouth was already watering.

"Don't mention it," she said. "Now, I'll need you seven days a week. Not all day of course but always on call. My client requests are time sensitive."

"Um, what would I be doing exactly?"

"Deliveries. Pick ups. Face time for clients. The usual."

My mind couldn't keep pace with the conversation. I was getting hired for a job I never applied for. Being someone's assistant just didn't seem like me. Especially for some well-connected Hollywood starlet. It was a better fit for some coffee-addicted college grad with dreams of mingling with celebrities.

"I can start you off at two thousand a week," she said.

"Two thousand? Seriously?" I couldn't hide my excitement.

Her phone rang. "Yes? Oh, that's too bad. Certainly. Bye." She stuck out her lower lip. "John canceled. Something came up at work."

I sank back in my chair. My shot at the graphic novel world crumbled away. The ascending bubbles in the celebratory champagne mocked me.

"Don't worry," Solas said. "I can still get it to him. Did you bring it?"

"Yeah."

Solas held out her hand. I retrieved the well-worn art pad from my messenger bag and passed it over.

She stared at the cover. "Foresight?"

"That's the hero's name."

She flipped through the pages, her eyes flitting over the artwork with a studied gaze. "What's his power?"

"He knows what an opponent thinks or does before it happens."

"Precognition." She answered automatically, her focus on the pages unbroken.

"Sort of. It's more like a constant three-second glimpse into the future."

She nodded. "Talk about déjà vu."

I laughed. "Yeah. At first he thinks he's losing his mind but once he learns to control it, he—"

"Who trains him?" she jumped in.

"Oh, um, this monk who—"

"An old man?"

"Yeah."

"Who happens to have the same powers, right?"

"Well ... yeah. How did you—"

"I told you, I work in Hollywood. I know story. Who's the villain?"

"She's a powerful shapeshifter made of flowing mist."

Solas stopped reading for a moment and looked up. "Your villain is a woman?"

"No offense," I said.

"None taken. Villains are usually the more intriguing character. Why should men have all the fun?" She gave a sly smile and continued on in the story. "Is this her?" She turned the art pad to face me. Her finger pointed to an action drawing of a beautiful, silver-haired woman in dark grey spandex. One of her arms was dissolving into mist as the hero tried to grab it.

"Yeah," I said.

"You know, most women don't have these kind of curvy proportions."

I paused a moment. "You do."

Solas smirked. "Quit staring." She closed the book and put it by her purse. "It has promise. I'll take it to John or one of my other clients. I'll make sure it gets in the right hands."

"Um, actually that's the original art. I should make a copy first."

"I'll take care of it." She sipped her champagne. "I work with a print service. It needs some tweaking before it meets submission guidelines."

"Oh, okay. That's great. How can I thank you?"

She lifted her glass toward me. "Do a good job as my assistant."

I grabbed my champagne and clinked our glasses together. "You got it."

Soon after, our filet mignon arrived with beautiful grill marks and a shiny glaze. The savory warmth of the steak washed over me straight from the kitchens of heaven. I grabbed my steak knife and dove right in.

It could have been the thrill of having my novel on it's way to publishers or the gorgeous woman sitting across from me but I couldn't remember the last time a meal tasted so good.

Her phone rang as I finished my last bite of paradise. After a quick chat, she returned the phone to her purse, threw a few hundreds on the table and stood.

"I have to go," she said. "My limo service is here."

I stood to say goodbye. "Must be nice."

"Amenities are a perk of my lifestyle. As my assistant, you'll find this translates to you as well." She reached into her purse and handed me a set of keys. "The 911 is now your company car. Try not to scratch it."

I stared at the dangling keys for a moment, afraid to touch them. "The Porsche? You want me to drive the Porsche?"

She nodded, grabbed my reluctant hand and placed them in my palm. "I'll have the Silver Towers retrieve your bike. It'll be there when you're done for the day."

I opened my palm just to make sure the keys were real. "This is great. Thank you."

She drew close and wrapped her arms around me as if she was my girlfriend. My lonely days had been piling up for many weeks now, so I didn't mind.

"Listen,"—she stared at me with her piercing blue eyes—"I see your talent. Stick with me and success is closer than you think. You've earned this. You deserve this. You just need to focus on yourself for awhile. Then good things will happen for you. Like this."

Solas leaned in and kissed me. It may have lasted for one second or one hour. I got a little dizzy, so it was hard to tell.

She drew back and smiled. "It'll be great working together. You'll see."

I couldn't think of any reason to disagree.

She walked away letting her fingers trace a line across my chin in the process. Her shimmering golden dress held my focus until she was out the door, then my attention drifted back to the keys in my hand. A ray of sunlight snuck through the foliage overhead and illuminated the Porsche logo on the keychain. The rearing stallion urged me to go past the speed limit. I couldn't believe my luck. Pricey steak lunch with a supermodel and now I was heading for one of the greatest cars ever made. It was like being a celebrity for a day.

I strode out of Magaris feeling the confident swagger of the rich and famous. The lustrous gold finish of the Porsche winked at me from the parking lot, promising an amazing drive.

Once I was snug in the form fitting leather seat with the engine purring, I had to take a moment and admire the interior. I was amazed to find the passenger seat free from any stains or water marks from my wet clothes last night. Frankly, it looked brand new. The car service at Silver Towers must've used some amazing restoration tricks.

With the air conditioner on full blast, I revved the engine

a few times for good measure and made the obligatory peel out from the parking lot.

I whisked through the streets of Long Beach wishing I was on some deserted mountain highway. The smooth steering wheel felt as though it was custom fitted for my hands. I laughed aloud, feeling the raw power beneath the gas pedal and my belly full of five star steak.

It was at that precise moment of bliss that the green-eyed menace appeared in the passenger seat.

CHAPTER 8

One moment I was alone in the car, a second later, old Green Eyes was sitting next to me. I jumped and let out a scream that was far less manly than I would have wanted anyone to hear.

Finch was dressed in a white sport coat and pants with a pink T-shirt. His hair had highlights, and his jawline sported a new five o' clock shadow.

"Nice car." He pulled a pair of ray bans from his coat pocket, shaded up and relaxed into the luxury seating. "Where'd you get it?"

"Hey, man." I tried to sound forceful, but my nerves were still jittery from his sudden appearance. "I don't know who you are or how you're doing all this, but I want you to leave me alone."

He puckered his lips like he was hurt. "You still don't believe me?"

"That you're an angel? No."

"Hm. I would've thought appearing next to you out of nowhere would've clinched it."

I was quiet for a moment. Whoever he was, he was able to do some bizarre things. Things I couldn't rationally explain. But to make the leap from that to him being an angel felt like admitting I was going crazy.

"Listen, Finch," I said.

"Finchelus."

"Whatever. No one has a name like that. I'm calling you *Finch*."

He crossed his arms and looked away. "Fine."

"I don't know what your game is, but you're really freaking me out."

"Well, maybe if you'd stop running away and ignoring my texts, we could start working together." He pulled down the sun shade and fixed his highlighted hair in the mirror.

"What's with the clothes?" I said. "You look ridiculous."

He slid his Ray Bans down. "Miami Vice. The coolest show around."

"No. Not cool. My mom watched that show."

"Oh, have it your way." He threw his shades on the floor in protest. "I'll wear terrible clothes from now on."

His white suit was instantly replaced by an Iron Man T-shirt and jeans. I grimaced realizing he was wearing my exact outfit.

"Happy?" he said.

I turned and stared blankly at the road ahead. Street signs glided by, and cars drove beside me as if the world was as normal and concrete as ever. But my world was leaving *normal* faster than the speed of the Porsche rumbling beneath me.

My excuses for who or what this guy was were failing. There was definitely something supernatural going on. Could this actually be an angel beside me?

"You sure don't act like an angel," I finally managed.

"Well, I'm not the typical field angel. They tend to use the well-spoken, diplomatic types. To be honest, after my snafu in 1985 and the resulting probation, I wasn't sure they'd send me down again. But when the call of duty comes, you gotta follow the big guy, am I right?" He gave me a light punch on the shoulder.

"Wait," I said. "You're on probation?"

He held up his hands. "Totally not my fault. My last assignment was classified as a DH4 but turned out to be far more like a DH9 to my sensibilities. It was really a case of poor identification. Frankly, I—"

"Hold on," I stopped him. "Why did they send me an angel on probation? What am I, some reject case?"

"Well, you are a DH6." He motioned ahead. "Watch the road."

Realizing I'd drifted in my distraction, I swerved back into my lane. "Why me? If I'm some charity case, why are you even here? I mean, a visit from an angel is pretty rare, right?"

"Eh, I don't analyze the *why*'s, that'll drive you crazy," Finch said. "I just do my job. DH6 or not, you asked God to do something great, and it looks like He's giving you a shot."

"Yeah, but it's not like I'm a pastor or missionary or anything. I have no power or influence, and I'm pretty much broke."

"All true. And a little sad." Finch sniffed and pretended to wipe a tear away. "But you have a willing heart. That's always the first step. Now you just have to follow through."

"With what?" I said. "What am I supposed to do?"

"First, stop running away from me. Next, continue with our missions. Something big is in the works, I can feel it. It's exciting to be a part of something worthwhile. Just prepare yourself. Any good effort encounters dark opposition."

Was he talking about evil spirits? And why would he mention them? "Wait, how do I really know you're an angel? Maybe *you're* a demon trying to trick me."

Finch smiled and pointed at me. "Aha. Not bad for a DH6. I'm proud of you. Okay, let's do this. I'm ready." He rubbed his hands together.

"Ready for what?"

He frowned. "You know. Hit me with the good stuff. Cast me out. Pray. Launch some scripture at me." Finch spread out his hands. "Come on, let it fly!"

"Um..." My mind was blank. "Really?"

Finch sighed. "If you were a soldier, would you go to battle without your weapons?"

My mind raced through fragmented bits of scriptures dealing with demons. Unfortunately, nothing helpful came to mind. The only thing I could do was send up a desperation prayer.

"All right. Here goes." I thought a silent prayer. It started a little shaky but eventually turned into a genuine plea for help. I was at a loss for what was going on and quite frankly, I needed a divine bail out. I finished with an amen spoken aloud.

He nodded. "Not bad. There was some real warmth in here. Enough to annoy a demon but probably not enough to lose one."

"All right, so what do I do? Tell you to leave, *Exorcist* style?"

"The robes and theatrics aren't necessary. Just the basics."

"Fine." I cleared my throat. "Get out of here, spirit."

He shook his head. "Demons aren't dogs. Call for backup."

"Okay. Get out of here by the power of God."

"Better. Be more specific."

"In the name of Jesus Christ, I order you to get out of here."

Finch gave a tooth-filled smile. "Now you're talking. Follow that up with some scripture and prayer, and you're on fire."

I paused. "But you're still here."

He spread out his hands. "Exactly. Now you know I'm not a demon."

Unfortunately I didn't know the Bible well enough to know if I was being conned. Still, besides his sometimes obnoxious personality, there was something about him that I wanted to trust. A gut feeling that he was telling the truth.

A homeless man sat against a run-down pawn shop ahead, his grimy dog curled up next to him. My attention snapped back to where I was. The storefronts had dated, sun-worn signs. Creeping trails of grunge marked their stucco exterior.

In my supernatural distraction, I'd ended up driving into a sketchy section of Long Beach. My golden Porsche stuck out like a sore thumb around here.

"Oh man," I said. "Time to make a U-turn."

"Why?" Finch said.

"We're headed into the hood. I don't want this Porsche jacked."

He scanned the street. "Looks okay to me. I'm guessing you've never been to a third world country."

"Whatever. I'm not taking any chances with this car." I pointed ahead. "Does that sign say no U-turn?"

A large white sign came into focus. The bright red circle and slash over the U-turn symbol looked like it was freshly painted.

"By the way," Finch said. "Where *did* you get this car? Your paperwork said nothing about it."

"It's kind of a company car. This woman hired me as an assistant."

"What woman?"

"I just met her. We really hit it off. She pays well, and I just run errands and stuff."

"Wait a second." Finch turned to me, his eyes narrowed. "When did you meet her?"

"Um, same night I met you."

"And she's sending you out on missions?"

"No. Errands."

Finch slumped back into his chair, his expression slack. "I don't believe this."

"What?" I said. "What's wrong with me getting a job? I need the money."

"They sent a backup." Finch spoke in a monotone. "They don't think I can handle it, so they sent a backup angel."

Picturing Solas as an angel made me laugh. "I don't think so, man. She's a little too..." I searched for the proper words to say to an angel.

"Too what?" he said.

"Sexy."

He huffed a laugh. "Well of course you're attracted to her. She's an angel. We're magnificent beings." He pointed to his hair. "Look at my highlights. Do you think any human hairstylist could achieve this perfection?"

"I don't know, Finch. I think it's just a coincidence."

He looked forward, his jaw tightening. "Trust me, she's an angel. This is an outrage. I am definitely talking to my superiors about this."

My head was starting to hurt. I couldn't talk about angels and demons anymore like it was a typical conversation. "Whatever. Fine, she's an angel. I gotta turn around and get out of here."

"Can you drop me off first?" he said.

"Here?"

"Yeah." He pointed to the next block. "Right up there is good."

"Why don't you just disappear? Can't you like, teleport or whatever?"

"Not now. Right here, you're going to miss my stop!"

"Okay, okay." I pulled over to the sidewalk.

I turned to say goodbye and the words caught in my throat. Instead of Finch wearing my same outfit, an old man wearing dusty, stain-covered clothes sat next to me. He turned to me and smiled. Several teeth were missing, and the ones that remained were stained yellow. Bright green eyes flashed for a moment, then faded to a pale blue.

"Pretty convincing, huh?" he said.

I nodded, unable to speak.

He looked out the side window. "Here she comes. Don't worry, I'll talk you up. Score some points for you."

"Wait, what?" I said.

He opened the door and stepped out. "Hello, pretty lady." He spoke in a shaky, old voice.

I opened the door and stepped out to see who he was talking to. I did a doubletake. Amber, my neighbor, was standing right next to him.

"Chris?" Her eyebrow raised.

"Amber. Hey."

"You made it." She smiled. "I wasn't sure you'd come."

I looked up to find the Caring Tables soup kitchen sign directly above her.

CHAPTER 9

◆

Somehow I had ended up smack dab in front of the Caring Tables soup kitchen. Was it a coincidence? Did Finch trick me? I looked over at my quick-change artist angel who now resembled a homeless old man.

"This nice young man brought me here...," Homeless Finch told Amber in his crotchety voice. "Said you had food for those in need."

"Of course," Amber said. "Lunch is right inside. What's your name?"

"Folks call me Finchelus." He turned to me and winked.

"Nice to meet you, Finchelus." Amber pointed him toward the front door.

Finch hobbled inside, and Amber turned to me.

"Nice car," she said. "You win the lottery?"

"It's kind of my new company car," I said.

"Wow. What company? Maybe I should submit a resume."

"It's a personal assistant thing. My boss is loaded. She has me running deliveries and stuff."

She looked up and down the street. "Well, you might want to park out back and cover it."

"Good thinking." I got back in and headed for the rear parking lot.

No backing out now. I guess I was volunteering this afternoon. After all, I did basically promise I would help out. Sweating over soup kettles wasn't an appealing thought, but spending time with Amber helped sweeten the deal.

I found a good place to park near the back entrance. Luckily there was a car cover behind the driver seat, and once I rolled it out, I was relieved to find it free of giant Porsche logos.

Amber met me at the back entrance. A knee length brown apron with Caring Tables printed in yellow lettering covered her cowgirl look. Her hair was tied back with a few escaped strands meandering down her face. Perspiration on her forehead told me she'd either been working hard or hovering over steaming soup pots or maybe both.

"I'm glad you made it." She was more energized than I'd ever seen her. It was as if she was headed to her favorite concert rather than a soup kitchen.

"Yeah. Sorry about the car." I jerked a thumb back. "It's probably kind of obnoxious to show up in something like that. Next time I'll bring my bike."

"Let's just hope it doesn't get keyed." She pulled at my forearm. "Come on, I'll show you around."

I gave a desperate glance back, vowing silently to check on the Porsche every five minutes.

"That was nice of you to give Finchelus a ride," she said. "Sometimes just getting here is half the battle."

"It was nothing." If she only knew.

Live music flowed down the hallway. Someone was playing an acoustic guitar and singing. It was an indie style tune somewhere between Jack Johnson and Ed Sheeran.

Inside the humble storefront was a main area set up like a buffet. A narrow hall led from there to a couple offices and bathrooms. The main area was filled with sturdy tables and chairs, half of which were occupied by homeless hunkered over their lunch trays. The tables had blue and white checkered cloths and artificial flower centerpieces. It was a combination of mess hall and country diner.

A guy in his early twenties wearing a plaid shirt and skinny jeans sat on a stool in the corner playing acoustic guitar. He had long blonde hair pulled back in a man bun. His hightop clad foot was wrapped in a leather collar with bells attached, which looked like it belonged around the neck of Santa's reindeer. He kept rhythm with his foot, causing the bells to jingle in time with the music.

"A soup kitchen with live music?" I said.

Amber chuckled. "That's Heath. He just got back."

"From being on tour?"

She smiled and shook her head. "C'mere, I'll introduce you."

Amber brought me over to the man-bun musician. We stopped a few feet in front of him and waited while he finished his tune. Heath kept his eyes closed as though lost in some musical spell while the last note faded away.

There was a smattering of applause from the homeless diners. Amber joined in on the applause, which seemed to break him out of his song haze.

Heath cast a mellow smile at Amber as though he just woke from a pleasant dream. "Hey. Am I too loud over here?"

"No, you sound great," she said. "Is that a new one?"

He nodded. "I wrote it during our Guatemala trip."

Uh-oh. Long distance trips together? Ex-boyfriend?

"Really?" she said. "You never played it for me."

"Yeah, I didn't want you to think I just used our time together for a love song."

She smiled as though touched.
Obviously this loser had to go. Soon.
"Chris." She turned back to me. "This is Heath. One of our regular volunteers. He just got back from Costa Rica."
"Hey, Chris." Heath leaned over his guitar, hand extended in my direction.
"Hey." I took hold of his hand wishing I could hammer-throw him back to Costa Rica. "So, do you record albums and stuff?"
"Nah,"—he waved me off—"I met with some label guys last year. Wanted to get me in the studio, go on tour, all that jazz."
"They offered him a two-album deal." Amber sounded a little too much like a proud girlfriend.
"But it just wasn't my scene. Felt like a sell out." He detached the reindeer bells from his shoe and stood. He had me by four inches, clocking in at around six foot two. "My music comes from inspiration not album deadlines."
I couldn't imagine turning down a deal to get paid to do something you loved. If I was offered a graphic novel contract, I'd find a way to make it work without "selling out." The way I looked at it, the chance to make a living pursuing your art was the chance to work full time perfecting a skill you loved while at the same time avoiding early death in an office cubicle.
"Well, you gotta keep your art pure, right?" Jealousy overtook my lips, encouraging him down the path of penniless musician and away from Amber's heart.
Heath nodded and propped his guitar on a stand. "Well, I should get back to the lunch line. Gwen probably needs a break."
"Good idea," Amber said. "Come on, Chris. I'll introduce you."
Amber pointed to a serving counter that extended out from the kitchen. "That's the lunch line. Might be a good place to get your feet wet."

"Okay." Scooping out servings of food didn't sound so bad. Amber brought me to the line which, at the moment, was empty of lunch goers. It was manned by a sixty-ish looking tall guy with a neatly trimmed white beard and an older woman leaning against the counter as if she was about to pass out. Both wore brown aprons with the Caring Tables logo. Heath high-fived the older guy and started mumbling something about guitar chords.

The pleasant aroma of melted cheese swept over me. I noticed a nearly depleted tray of triangle-cut grilled cheese sandwiches. It took me back to lunchtime rainy days as a kid. For some reason I'd expected the putrid smell of some dark gruel. If I wasn't full of steak, I'd probably be asking for one.

"Greg, Gwen, this is Chris." Amber motioned to me.

"This my relief?" Gwen spoke with a lifetime-smokers voice.

Amber nodded.

"Great. I've got paperwork to do." Gwen took off her apron and handed it to me. "You're up slugger."

"Gwen heads up Caring Tables," Amber said. "Without her, this place would've closed years ago."

Gwen patted Amber's shoulder. "We made a good go of it. We'll ride it till the end, right?"

Amber nodded.

Gwen turned to me. "Stop by my office before you go. Fill out a volunteer form. Appreciate you coming in today." She flashed a brief smile, then headed toward the back office, a fresh Marlboro already between her fingers.

"Ride it till the end?" I said.

Amber frowned. "Financial stuff. It's tough to keep this place running."

I nodded. "I hear that."

"Well," Amber glanced at the apron in my hands then back at me. "You ready?"

"Yeah. Let's do this." I threw on the apron and pulled back the strings to tie it.

"I'll get that." Amber moved behind me, tying the apron in place.

I turned to thank her and ended up a little too close for a typical friend zone distance. She didn't move. The smallest hint of a smile turned the corner of her mouth. Her coffee-colored eyes held mine as if I were in a trance. I forgot for a moment where I was.

"How's your cheek today?" She lightly touched my bruised cheekbone.

"Oh, it's nothing. I'm fine." Her touch was like magic pouring through me.

Amber smiled. "Thanks again for coming, Chris. Maybe Heath or Greg can show you the ropes." She removed her apron and turned to leave.

"Wait," I said. "You're not staying?"

She shook her head. "No. Picked up an extra shift at the diner. I'm hoping to make back some of that stolen money."

"Oh. Okay." I felt like someone let the air out of my tires. The next couple hours would be all grilled cheese and man buns and no Amber. This was definitely not part of the plan.

Amber waved and a few seconds later she was out the door. There was a solid pat on my back. I turned to find Heath smiling his mellow musician smile at me.

"Come on," Heath said. "I'll bring you up to speed."

I smiled, but inside I was crying. I barely even got a chance to talk to Amber. Now I was stuck with her ex who she probably still had feelings for.

There was nothing I could do about it now. As long as I was here, I might as well get some solid volunteering done. At least handing out sandwiches wasn't that bad of a job.

I scanned the serving trays. Grilled cheese, apple sauce, rice, and salad.

"No soup?" I said.

Greg, the white-bearded volunteer behind the counter, turned to me, a grin animating the left side of his mouth. "You thought we only served soup here, didn't you?"

"No." I tried to think of something clever to counter my newbie vibe. "I just thought tomato soup would have been the obvious choice for grilled cheese."

He nodded like he almost bought my answer. "Well, the lunch rush is over. I can handle the stragglers if you two can tackle the dishes."

Dishes. The word seemed to hang in the air as my mind struggled with it's unavoidable implications. I imagined a dark basement piled high with old food calcified on silverware and slime trails of apple sauce dripping off plates.

"Sure." Heath slapped my back again which I was not a fan of. "How 'bout it, Chris?"

I forced a grin. "Okay."

Heath led the way to the back of the kitchen where an industrial-strength metal sink waited for us. The sink was flanked with stacks of dirtied plates already glued together with old cheese.

"Here." Heath tossed me a pair of yellow latex gloves.

We dug into the plate stacks. Heath showed mercy and took wash duty while I dried. He brandished one of those overhanging spray nozzles to power wash the plates.

The smell of soggy sink food hung in the air. But far worse was the combination of vanilla incense and patchouli oil seeping from Heath's musical pores.

"So,"—I searched for a conversation starter—"just back from Costa Rica?"

"Yeah. Spent a few months there," Heath said. "Waves are unreal."

"Ah. World-traveling surfer, huh? Are you sponsored and all that?"

He shrugged. "I have a few indie sponsors. I just go to hang with friends. Do some travel photography, maybe some charity work."

"Cool. Sounds expensive."

"We have a YouTube channel. The ads we run pay for most of it. The rest, my sponsors take care of."

"Not bad." He was like an entrepreneurial vagabond.

Heath stopped washing for a moment to take a deep stretch. "Missed yoga this morning. I'm totally locked."

"Never tried it," I said. "Probably why my drawing hand always cramps up."

He nodded like he was half listening, then started the spray nozzle back up. "It's weird to be back. Don't remember this place feeling so closed."

I wasn't sure how to respond. "The soup kitchen?"

"The whole place." He waved his hand around. "Ever since I got off the plane. All the buildings. The people. The air." He opened his mouth like he was going to say more, then went back to washing.

"Well, that's city life I guess."

"Yeah." He turned to me, his face tightened with concern. "The whole flow is off, right?"

He was losing me fast. It was like a bad case of hippie jet lag.

"Um," I said. "Are you talking like Chi and crystals and stuff?"

He shook his head. "No man. You're missing it. It's all just too uptight. The faces. The sidewalks. Everything is angular..." He stared at the wall for a moment as if he could see through it. "...I dunno. Forget it."

Gladly.

"So," I said, "you back for good or leaving on another surf trip soon?" Please say you're leaving. Please say you're leaving.

"I'm back for a little bit." An easy grin spread across his face. "It's good to see Amber again. I did miss her."

No. Bad. Wrong answer.

"Oh yeah?" I tried to stay relaxed. "You guys have a thing going?"

"We used to. I miss her." He turned to me with a smile. "She's great, isn't she?"

I nodded, trying to appear nonchalant. "Sure. Great."

"Yeah. We got some serious catching up to do, me and her."

All I could think about was turning that spray nozzle on his face.

"Oh, man. You know what?" He turned to me, his mouth slightly open in the most lazy attempt at surprise I'd ever seen. "I forgot my buddy is waiting for me. Gotta pick up his Djembe at Monks Music Hut."

"His what?"

"Hand drum." He peeled off his yellow gloves causing an elastic snap. "Bro, can you snag the rest of these for me?"

With wide eyes of shock I surveyed the remaining mounds of dishes. "Oh, dude. I don't know. I—"

He slapped me on the back. "Thanks bro. Totally appreciate it."

And just like that he was trotting out of the kitchen, his man bun lightly bouncing against his head with each step.

A heavy brick of despair settled in my chest. What could I do? I assumed his spot at the spray nozzle and got to work.

By mid afternoon I was back in the Porsche. Over an hour of cleaning cheese and partially dried applesauce off plates was maximum strength volunteer work in my book. True, I wasn't bringing aid to lepers in Calcutta, but still, it was a pretty gnarly job.

Truth be told, even with the horrible Heath experience, I felt better than I had in months. There was a deep sense of fulfillment after volunteering. Part of me was excited I'd committed a full week of lunch duty to this place. The other part wanted to get back to steak with supermodels. Obviously, this would be an ongoing mental battle.

I started the Porsche's glorious engine and checked my messages. There were three texts from Solas, each about fifteen minutes apart.

> Can you head to 217 Glendarin St? Need a package pickup. Tell them you're with Ms. Callow.

> Chris, did you get my last text? Please respond.

> Client is getting antsy. Please tell me you're on your way.

My heart sank. I forgot I'd turned off the phone after Finch kept texting me. My new job just started, and I'd already screwed it up. I sent back a quick text.

> Sorry, ringer was off. On my way.

I plugged the address into my phone and zipped the Porsche back on the road. The address took me down to a row of warehouses near the the port.

Driving into the port of Long Beach was like arriving for an interstellar work assignment on an alien planet. Rows of mammoth steel cranes moved metal containers on and off cargo ships all day. The stacks of multi-colored containers around the port looked like neatly stacked Legos waiting for a giant child to come and smash it all to pieces. Everything just seemed too big for an average-sized human to be a part of.

I stopped outside an off white warehouse with no windows in the front. Other than a grey, metal door flanked by metal numbers signifying the address, the building was a large, non-descript box.

The Porsche fit into the last open parking space by the front entrance, the performance tires crunching against sun-bleached gravel.

I stepped outside the car and scanned the row of unadorned warehouse buildings. The street was deserted. I wondered if I was in the right place. A dog bark echoed in the distance, the only sound other than my feet against the gravel. It was the kind of lonely, shadow-filled place I wouldn't want to be at night.

A raised voice came from inside the building. I listened for a moment, but it was gone as quick as it had broken the silence. Another glance at my phone and the address on the building verified the match. I was at the right place ... apparently.

Several gruff voices echoed from the far end of the street. The sound grew louder as if the guys speaking were approaching. The next warehouse over blocked my view of who they were, but my guess was I had about thirty seconds before they arrived. I imagined a group of burly longshoreman, cranky from a long day of work, all too ready to take out their frustration on a comic book nerd with a Porsche.

I shut the car door, set the alarm, and hurried to the front of the warehouse. Better to take my chances with whoever was inside. At least they were expecting me.

Before I could even knock, the door swung open with a metal squeak. A squat guy with a beer belly and a birds nest of brown curly black hair stood there. A disheveled blue suit rested sideways on his paunchy frame as if he'd slept in it.

"Yeah?" he said.

"Hi. I'm here for a package," I said. "Ms. Callow sent me."
He studied my face a moment. "You a cop?"
"What? No."
He pointed a finger at me. "You the guy that's been asking questions at Reggies?"
I held up my hands as if his finger was a gun. "Dude, no. I don't even know Reggie. Ms. Callow gave me this address."
"Don't lie to me." He stepped closer, his pointing finger digging into my chest. "You got cop stink all over you."
My head was spinning. I felt like bolting for the Porsche. "No, man. Trust me. I don't even know any cops."
He reached deep into his jacket pocket. "That's it. Now I know you're lying."
"Dude, I swear." I held my hands forward as if they could block whatever deadly weapon he was about to pull.
He threw his head back, laughing hysterically. "I'm kidding," he gasped. "Oh man, I had you on the ropes."
Laughter from several other men came from inside the building.
He looked toward the sound of laugher inside and jerked his thumb at me. "Did you see this kid? Hope he's wearing a diaper."
The laughter inside swelled.
I gritted my teeth, frustrated at being the butt of his prank. "Very funny."
"Hey, no harm meant." He slapped my shoulder and laughed. "I always razz the new guys. What's your name?"
I thought back to the gym trainer and the folly of giving out my real name. Especially in a situation like this. "Harry."
He motioned to his chest. "Hey, my name's Harry, too. But everyone calls me Bender. Come on in."
Bender led me into a bare warehouse with a few sturdy metal work tables set up on the far side of the room. The tables were piled with consumer electronics—tablets, cell

phones, and flat screens here and there. A handful of younger guys worked at the tables using soldering guns and thin tools. It felt like the tech department at an electronics store.

The droning sound of an industrial strength A/C unit reverberated from the ventilation system. They must've had the air conditioner at full tilt because the place felt like a refrigerator, especially after coming in from the late summer heat.

"Hey everybody," Bender called. "This is Harry. The new guy."

Bender's announcement was mainly directed at three husky guys in grey jump suits seated at a round table separating us from the electronic work stations beyond. The biggest guy with black, slicked-back hair was reading the newspaper, the other two were sipping from styrofoam cups.

"Hey, new guy." One of the jump-suit guys with a shaved head lifted his cup.

The other guy sipping from a cup narrowed his eyes at me. He wore a Dodgers cap pulled low. "I give him two weeks."

Shaved Head coughed out a laugh. "Yeah. I say one and a half."

"Shut up." The guy with the newspaper didn't even bother to look up. "Package is next to Trench." He ticked his head toward the metal workstations.

"Come on. I'll show you." Bender led me to the closest workstation. A big guy with tattoos covering his arms worked on the circuit board of a laptop. A black visor with magnification lenses covered the top of his head. Apparently, this was Trench.

Bender grabbed a shoe box-sized package wrapped in brown paper and handed it to me. "There you go, Harry." He glanced at Trench who was still focused on the circuit board, then back to me. "You wanna meet some of the boys?"

My focus zeroed in on the tattoos covering Trench's arm. They were strangely familiar. A menagerie of skulls, snakes, and skeletons. Fresh scratch marks trailed down his forearm. Recognition hit me like a cold bullet.

This guy was the wife beater-wearing thug from the ATM robbery.

CHAPTER 10

A jolt of panic like an electrical charge surged through my chest. Bender was about to introduce me to the thug whose robbery I had stopped. The thug that knocked me to the ground. With my face still bearing the mark of his last attack, I might as well have a sign that said, "Remember me? Why don't you finish that beating you started last night?"

I spun, putting my back to Trench in case he looked up. I could imagine him shooting eye beams at me from his magnification goggles."

"No thanks, I can't stay," I said to Bender. "I gotta go. Wait, I got a call." I grabbed my phone with my free hand and stuck it to the side of my face closest to Trench in order to further hide my identity.

"What's the hurry?" Bender sounded a little annoyed.

"Sorry, man. Important call." I strode toward the front door trying not to look like I was running away.

"I told you." The skinhead in the jumpsuit pointed to me as I passed. "A week and a half. Tops."

I could care less what bet I was a part of with the table of jumpsuit idiots. I needed to get out of there before things escalated. Thankfully, I was out the door and headed to the Porsche without anyone stopping me.

A feeling of being watched came over me. I stopped a few feet from the car and looked across the street.

Something was there.

Shadows moved inside the building on the opposite side of the street. An abandoned factory, apparently. Remnants of chipped paint clung to the exterior. Rows of windows dotted the building face. A layer of grime covered the glass, obscuring the movement within.

I strained to make out who or what was inside the building. Dark shapes gathered near the windows. Their eyes were on me. Dull, grey eyes. There was a faint glow about them, like a bulb that was about to go out.

They were human in form, but something wasn't quite right. Whenever they moved, it was as if they were made of liquid. If the sun was low enough, I could've written them off as a trick of the eye. But that wasn't the case, so I couldn't use that explanation. No denying their existence.

A chill crept over my skin. I hugged my arms for warmth, all the while realizing it was mid afternoon on a hot September day. The dark forms pressed against the windows as though they wanted to break through. They were silent, but I couldn't shake a sense of malice directed toward me. As much as I didn't want to admit it, I knew they weren't human. They couldn't be. Deep down I sensed these things were supernatural.

My skin was buzzing with anxiety. I didn't want to look at them anymore. I wanted to run.

The front door of the abandoned building jostled on it's hinges as though something inside had slammed against it. The door settled, then shook from impact once again, this time with greater force. Someone or something was trying to get out. My fingers clutched the keys in my pocket. Time to go.

My body was leaden with fear, as if I was in a dream where I couldn't run. I forced myself to turn away from the old building and lunged toward the car.

I tossed the package on the passenger seat and managed to calm my shaky hands enough to start the engine. Gravel spit behind the tires as I floored it outta there.

My breathing pattern didn't return to normal till I was elevated onto the Vincent Thomas Bridge. From this high vantage point, the gargantuan cranes and containers of the port almost seemed normal-sized. I let out a long breath, relieved to be free of the warehouse of death.

I had no idea what I'd just experienced, but I definitely didn't want seconds. Whatever supernatural connections were happening to me had gone too far. I wanted out.

Not only that, but why would Solas send me there? Did I just leave some illegal electronics ring? And what on earth was Trench, the ATM tattoo thug, doing there? Maybe I should call the cops and report him. Although, with my call to the police last night about Finch, they probably had put me on some paranoid callers list. Who knew if they would even respond this time?

My head hurt. It was time for a recharge at home.

The apartment was a sweltering hole. When I opened the front door, a thick wave of heat hit me. Wearing shorts and an undershirt, Steve kneeled about a foot from a box fan. His long hair was free from it's pony tail, and the fan was whipping it around his face. He was in the middle of putting art supplies in a canvas carrying case.

"Is our apartment on fire?" I said.

Steve lifted a perspiring glass of ice water to his forehead. "Heater broke. It won't shut off. The super said he'd come check it out sometime today."

I took a few steps inside and felt dizzy. The suffocating air made it difficult to breathe. "This is unreal. It's like hell in here."

Steve nodded. "I'm grabbing supplies so I can get outta here. I'm headed to the studio to work."

The "studio" was a storage room near the art department at Long Beach State. They left it open most of the time for art students to paint and sculpt and talk about how no one understands them.

"You're leaving?" My voice sounded more desperate than I intended. "I need to talk to you."

"Here? We'll melt."

"Let's grab coffee."

He arched a brow.

"Iced coffee," I said.

"I'm always up for talking, but I've got plans." Steve snapped his case closed and stood. "I promised Julie I'd meet her at the studio. She's working on Cubism, but it's looking more like cave painting."

"I thought she was back with her boyfriend," I said.

Steve grinned. "It didn't stick." He threw on a short sleeve button-up shirt and headed for the door.

"Wait." I stopped him. My world was sideways. I needed advice big time. "It's important."

He studied my face a moment. "Is this about your 'paranormia?'" Steve used exaggerated air quotes to mock me.

I hesitated.

He shook his head and moved past me. "Forget it."

"Hold on." I grabbed his art case, cutting his departure short. "I'll drive you."

"On the back of your bike? No thanks."

"No." I jingled the Porsche key ring. "We'll ride in style." Steve held onto his skeptical face all the way to the street until I hit the car alarm and opened the passenger door for him.

"Whose car is this?" he said.

"Solas, my new boss," I said. "The supermodel from last night."

A crinkle line formed on his forehead. "You're really losing it, aren't you? Did you steal this?"

"Course not. Get in."

Steve put his canvas bag in the back. "Whatever. If the cops pull you over, I don't know anything about it."

We got in, and Steve picked up the package I'd left on his seat.

"What's this?" he said.

I started the beautiful engine. "That's my new job. Pickups and deliveries."

He turned the package over. "There's no label. What's inside?"

"No idea." I pulled the Porsche onto the street, adding a tire squeal for good measure.

Steve clutched the hand rest. "Easy, speedy. This car is awesome, but I don't want to die in it."

I smirked and took the next turn a little too fast, making the tires chirp.

He shook his head and went back to inspecting the package. "So, that woman is paying you to deliver unmarked packages around town?"

"Yep," I said. "Good money, too. In a couple weeks, not only will I have rent, but I can afford that self-publishing package for my graphic novel. But I might not even need it. Solas is hooking me up with big players in the publishing industry."

"Seems like she's doing a lot for someone she just met. Maybe these deliveries are illegal."

"Oh, come on."

"Well, how do you know? Where'd you pick this up? Did the place seem legit?"

I was silent for a moment wondering how I could possibly put a positive spin on the warehouse of shifty thugs and neighborhood demons.

"Uh-huh." Steve gave a tight lipped grin like my silence confirmed his theory. "Man, for all you know this package is filled with cocaine."

"Cocaine?" I laughed. "You watch too many movies."

"Suit yourself." He put the package on the floor of the back seat. "I want nothing to do with it. You need to ask that woman for details. Otherwise, if you get caught transporting illegal stuff, she'll pin it all on you."

"Fine. I'll ask. I'm sure it's all legit." As confident as I tried to sound, Steve was freaking me out a little. That warehouse was enough to make me question what I'd gotten involved in. Once I dropped Steve off, I'd put in a call to Solas.

Soon we were cruising down Seventh Street headed for Long Beach State.

"What do you know about angels?" I decided to jump right into the awkward questions that were eating at me. Plus, it distracted from the package conversation.

Steve kept his expression neutral. "I've never read a verse where they wear eighties clothes."

"Very funny. Didn't they sometimes walk among people? You know, in biblical times. With robes and sandals and stuff."

"Yeah."

"Well, they'd have to update their clothes with the times, right?"

"Look man," Steve started talking with his hands which usually meant he was losing patience with me. "I'm no theologian, but from what I know, the Bible doesn't give a lot of details about angels. They definitely have power but mostly they're messengers. The guy you described from last night sounds like a lunatic."

"Well, he's not a typical field angel. Actually, he's on probation. Last time he was here was the eighties so he's kind of stuck in old styles and..." I paused, realizing Steve was raising his eyebrows at me. "Never mind. Listen, the guy can appear out of nowhere. He can change his look in a second. Not just outfits, he can age fifty years in the blink of an eye."

I could tell Steve was in doubt mode, but I didn't care, I had to let it out.

"And he's not the only thing," I said. "I'm seeing weird shadows lurking around, and there's a serious creepy vibe when they're close. I think they're demons or something. I'm not imagining all this."

Steve let out a long sigh. "Man, I don't know what to tell you. Maybe that guy is a hypnotist. Maybe he's giving you hypnotic suggestions and it all seems real."

"No. I'm fully awake. You do believe in angels and demons, right?"

"Yeah, but—"

"I'm looking to you for spiritual guidance. You know the Bible more than me."

"I've been a Christian for ten years," he said. "That doesn't make me an expert on the supernatural realm."

"Well, you're the best I've got. Just tell me, if you were in my situation, what would you do?"

Steve let out a long breath and sat back in the leather seat. He was quiet for several moments. "Well, I'd pray a lot. You don't mess with the supernatural. There's powerful forces at work. I wouldn't trust anything that didn't line up with the Bible." He looked toward the back seat. "Like delivering cocaine."

"It's not cocaine!" I said.

My phone buzzed, and I took a quick glance. A new text spread across the screen.

I handed the phone to Steve. "Here. Read that to me."

Steve held it close. "*Thanks for the pickup today.*" He put the phone down. "This your hot boss?"

"Yes. Keep reading."

"*Client worried by your nervous behavior.*" He looked over. "Why were you nervous? Sketchy pickup spot, right?"

"Just read it!"

"*Going to an award show tonight. Lots of industry people that might be interested in your novel. Meet me at the Shrine Auditorium at 7. Wear the Armani.*" Steve looked up like he just ate a lemon. "Porsches? Award shows? Who are you?"

"Ugh." The awards show scared me more than a thug filled warehouse. It was one of those things I'd put on my anti-bucket list. I had no idea how to play the phony, self-important networking game, nor did I want to learn. "Do I have to go to this?"

"If it goes against who you are, don't do it."

"What about the industry people?" I said. "Maybe this is my shot."

"Is this how you want it to happen?"

I shrugged. "Maybe this is how it works."

Steve was quiet for a few moments. "Listen, you've got a lot going on, and I'm not even talking about your angel visions. You're obviously stressed. At least let me pray for you."

As I turned onto the college campus, Steve prayed. He kept using words like clarity, discernment, and wisdom. It was encouraging at first, but as the prayer continued it seemed like he was praying for someone who wasn't too bright.

I pulled up to the curb next to the art department. "You know that prayer was a little insulting."

Steve held up his hands. "No offense, man. Just want to make sure you're thinking clearly." He got out and retrieved his art case. Before he left, he leaned into the car. "Just remember, if you are dealing with something supernatural, you better grab onto your faith and hold tight. Remember how we learned Psalm 23 in college group? The Lord is my shepherd and all that?"

"Yeah?" I said.

He pointed at me. "Keep it handy. It's a strong one for spiritual warfare. See you tonight."

Steve shut the door and headed off to the studio. I sat there a few moments, picturing myself mingling with celebrities at an award show. I might as well have been headed to Mars to meet aliens.

CHAPTER 11

After a double bacon cheeseburger with onion rings, I achieved temporary inner peace. I pushed thoughts of glitzy award shows out of my head and focused on the familiar, comforting streets of Long Beach.

Pacific Coast Highway spun me into the traffic circle—the intersection of three major streets and a testing ground for beginning drivers. I did an extra loop on the inside lane to fully appreciate the performance handling of the Porsche, then floored it out of the circle and headed home.

Back at my apartment, the door opened and a thick blanket of heat descended. Apparently the super was taking his time with the heater repair, or as occasional late rent payers, we were at the bottom of his priority list.

The sound of footsteps heading up the stairway caught my attention. Amber came into view, clad in her server uniform.

She smiled as our eyes met. "Hi, Chris."

"Hey. How'd you do tonight?"

Amber passed her apartment door and headed toward me.

"I broke a hundred. Another seven shifts like this, and I'll pay off that stolen money."

To me it was kind of a depressing thought, but she was obviously more of an optimist. Maybe if I hung around her enough, it would rub off. "Nice."

She peered into my apartment. "Why are you standing outside?"

"Heater's broke. It's an oven in there."

She leaned in and immediately recoiled. "Wow. And what's that smell?"

Unfortunately the smell was pre-heat wave but it made for a good excuse.

"Yeah." I waved a hand in front of my face. "Steve probably left some food out."

"Did you call the super?"

I nodded. "I don't think he likes us."

Amber chuckled. "So, you're just gonna stand out here all night?"

"Maybe."

She grabbed my arm. "Come on. I can't leave you in the hallway."

As Amber led me to her apartment door, I couldn't help but remember just last night when my fumbled attempt to flirt sent her rushing into her apartment to bolt-lock the door. Now here she was inviting me in. It was a fantastic turn of events, and I couldn't help but feel somewhat grateful that my heater broke.

Her apartment was a mess. A stack of dirty dishes leaned out of the kitchen sink, Post-its with random notes clustered around the phone and spread over the counter like a growing virus, and a trail of clothes led to a bedroom that seemed to be carpeted in shoes. It definitely wasn't the tidy, spa retreat I'd imagined.

She turned to me, narrowing her eyes. "Don't say a word."

I put out my hands like I hadn't noticed a thing. "What?"

"I've been too busy working at the diner and helping at Caring Tables. Something had to give."

"Hey, it's not a hundred degrees in here, and I get to hang out with you. No complaints."

A slow smile spread across her face. "You hungry?" She made her way to the kitchen, grabbing an old pizza box and trashing it in the process. "I was gonna make tacos."

"Didn't you just come from a restaurant?"

"Blech. No thank you. I'm around their food twenty-four seven. Plus, I love to cook for people. It's one of the reasons I'm going to culinary school."

My stomach was packed with bacon cheeseburger heaven, but how could I refuse? She was going to cook dinner for me. As far as I understood relationship signals, that was huge. "Sure. I love tacos."

I wandered toward the humble living room that seemed more frat house than beauty queen. A brown futon faced off against a glass coffee table and a flat screen the size of a briefcase.

"Oh." She turned. "How was the soup kitchen?"

"Good." I nodded. "I was a little nervous at first. I'm not like a big volunteer guy or anything, but it was cool. Really makes you feel like you're making a difference, you know?"

Her shoulders dropped as her whole body seemed to relax. "That's awesome, Chris." She smiled and turned to the fridge, pulling out food for the tacos. "Did Heath show you around?"

The mention of his name started my eye twitching. "Kind of. We started on dishes together, but then he bailed. Something about a hand drum."

"Musicians." She chuckled like it was cute that he left me stranded. "Easily distracted, but he's a real sweetheart where it counts."

"Mm." I really wanted to argue that point, but what could I say? "He said you guys used to date?"

Up until that moment I'd decided not to bring up their past relationship. It was almost never good to get the woman you're falling for, thinking about their last boyfriend. Especially when he's back in town singing a brand new batch of love songs. But my jealousy overtook my brain, and somehow I just blurted out the words.

"Yeah. Last summer." She grabbed some ground beef from the fridge and put it on the counter. "Things ended a little weird."

Weird. That sounded like something I could use.

"Oh yeah?" I said. "Well, he does talk in that pothead poetry kind of way."

"Chris!" She said my name like she intended to scold me but couldn't hold back a laugh.

"Sorry." I held up my hands. "He's just a little out there for me."

"He's an artist," she shrugged. "When you write lyrics, you see the world in poetic ways."

This wasn't going well. If I kept bringing up character defects that she would spin into beautiful brilliance, I might as well set them up on a date to rekindle lost love. Maybe it was better to just ask her.

"So, what happened with you guys?" I said.

"Timing, I guess." Amber placed the ground beef on the skillet, and it started to sizzle. "Maybe I overthought the whole thing. He was always getting together with musicians, making videos, setting up surf trips, and all that. It's totally fine, I know that's his thing, it's just ... there were so many distractions."

"He sounds kind of flaky," I said.

She gave me a scolding look before continuing. "Anyway, sometimes I just wanted to take a break from it all and do the simple stuff. Watch a movie, grab coffee, that kind of thing." She picked up a tomato and started chopping it on the cutting board with chef-like speed and precision.

"Didn't you go with him?" I said. "On the trips, I mean."

"Sometimes," she said. "We went to Guatemala for two weeks. Part vacation, part mission trip. It was amazing." Her face lit up with a broad smile.

Why on earth did I bring this up? I might as well call Heath and ask him to come over and take my place.

"But the day we got back," she continued, "one of his sponsors called. A three week trip to Cancun. He didn't even unpack. He just called up his surf buddies and said he'd miss me."

"Oh." This part of the story sounded much better. "He didn't ask you to go?"

She shook her head. "I wouldn't have gone anyway. We just got back. I wanted to get to work in the soup kitchen. And I didn't want to lose my job. Besides, I missed home."

"Sounds like Heath is more of a 'home is where your suitcase is' kind of guy." It felt good to get a jab into their tale of romance.

"Who knows," she said. "Maybe he'll stick around this time."

I winced. Did she sound hopeful? Doubtful? It was hard to tell. Maybe it was time to change the subject.

"Well, I'm sure the people at Caring Tables are glad you stuck around. I think what you're doing there is awesome. You're changing peoples lives."

"I hope so," she said. "I'm praying we can stay afloat. The kitchen is pretty short on funds lately."

"You mean the money those thugs stole from you?" For a moment I considered bringing up my sighting of Trench, the ATM thug, but I couldn't figure out a good way to explain it.

She shook her head. "That was just the nail in the coffin. An inspector showed up a few months ago. The kitchen wasn't up to code. Issues with the wiring, plumbing, random repairs—the list was crazy. We're still not finished with everything, but we're out of money." She leaned forward on the kitchen counter. "You don't have forty thousand dollars lying around do you?"

If she only knew how broke I was. "I could start playing the lottery."

"You and me both," she said.

I zeroed in on a waist-high DVD case that bordered the kitchen and living room. I figured it was a good time to lighten the mood. "DVDs, huh? No Netflix?"

"Yeah, guess I'm old school." She chuckled.

A quick scan revealed a potpourri of romantic comedies, Disney animated movies, the obligatory *Titanic* DVD, and a sprinkling of heavier dramas like *Schindler's List* and *Casablanca*.

Amber was busy grabbing more taco ingredients from the refrigerator.

"I don't see any superhero movies in your collection," I said.

"Ugh," she said. "No thank you."

A small chink formed in her perfect-girl armor.

"How 'bout sci-fi?" I braced for impact.

She started scooping half an avocado out of it's shell. "Boring."

Amber was wounding me pretty bad. I scanned the movie collection once more, hoping to stop the bleeding. "Aha. I see *Back to the Future*."

"So?"

"Time-traveling machines and eccentric scientists? That's classic sci-fi."

A crinkle formed between her eyes. "Really?"

"Yeah." My hope was returning. I found another familiar title on the bottom row, and a thrill went through me . "And you have *Iron Man*. That's sci-fi *and* superhero."

"That was a gift."

"Oh."

"But I do like it," she said. "Robert Downey Jr. is funny. And easy on the eyes."

Terrific. Now I was competing with Heath and Iron Man. Once again, it was time to change the subject. "Need any help over there?"

A small grin turned up the corner of her mouth as if she was hoping I'd ask. "Sure. Grab the taco shells."

We spent the next fifteen minutes cooking together and setting the table to eat. Conversation was so effortless it felt like we'd been friends for years. I'd become so used to awkward conversations with women lately, it was like finding an oasis in the desert.

She used ingredients and spices in her cooking like an alchemist whipping up potions. There was fresh guacamole and mango salsa made from scratch. I went through about a dozen chips doing taste tests because it was so delicious. Amber finally had to take the chips and hide them from me.

Everything smelled so amazing when she finished, my appetite cried for a do over, and I regretted filling my stomach an hour ago.

"Where'd you learn to cook like this?" I said.

"My grandpa. He ran a Mexican food spot downtown about the size of this apartment." She smiled as if lost in a memory. "I helped my mom out in the kitchen when I was only seven. Loved it ever since."

I grabbed a plate with two tacos. "Well, if the smell is any clue, these are gonna be awesome."

The tacos were the kind of meal that's so incredible, you forgot about your problems and the stress melted away for a few enjoyable moments. I leaned back when I was done and let out a contented sigh.

"You want another taco?" Amber said.

I held up my hands. "No."

Her brow lifted a bit. I'd only eaten two tacos, so she probably took it as a cooking insult.

"It was awesome," I quickly added. "Seriously, I watched everything you did, and I don't understand how it came out that good without magic. I ate a little earlier or else I'd have like ten of them."

"Oh. You should have told me you already ate."

"And miss out on dinner with you? No way."

She smiled, her eyes locked onto mine a few moments. "I'm glad you were here tonight, Chris."

"Me too."

My phone buzzed. A new text from Solas filled the screen.

> Where are you? The show started fifteen minutes ago.

"Sorry." I glanced at Amber. "It's my new boss. I have to answer this."

Amber nodded and started collecting dishes as I tapped out a response

> Thanks for the invite but I can't make it.

The phone was almost back in my pocket when it buzzed again.

> Part of your job is to be on call. I need that package tonight, and I was going to connect you with industry people as a personal favor.

I let out a long sigh.

"What's wrong?" Amber said.

"Oh, my new boss invited me to this thing, and I didn't go."

"A work thing?" she said.

I shrugged. "I don't know. I'm either an on-call assistant or a delivery boy. It's really fuzzy."

"Maybe you should go."

"Nah." The last thing I wanted to do was leave Amber and drive to L.A. for an awards show. Plus, I needed to know just what kind of package delivery I was involved in. I tapped out a quick response.

> Pickup spot was sketchy today. Need to talk to you about that. Can't make it to L.A. tonight. I'll drop package at Silver Towers. I'll give it to the concierge.

A response came so fast I couldn't even put the phone down.

> No. Meet me at 8 for breakfast at Novel Crepes. Bring the package.

I stared at the screen for a moment, then turned the phone off and stuffed it in my pocket. "All settled. I'm not going."

"Really?" Amber said. "It's okay if you have to go. I have to run another errand before bed anyway."

"ATM?"

Her eyes narrowed. "No. Laundromat."

"Need a ride?"

She waved me off. "That's okay. It's not the most exciting place."

"I don't mind." I pulled out the Porsche keys. "And we can go in style."

"You sure?"

"Yeah. Plus it will help clean this place up, so it's kind of necessary."

She grabbed the hot sauce bottle and lifted it up. "Don't make me hurt you."

Soon we were in the Porsche headed down Atlantic Street toward the laundromat. Her overstuffed hamper leaned across the back seat, spilling clothes onto the floor mat where my unmarked package crouched in the shadows, waiting for delivery.

Amber rubbed the leather seat. "I can't believe this is your company car. It's so nice."

"I know, it's crazy. I need to find a deserted cliff-side highway like the commercials."

"Wait." She pointed to a street we just passed. "The laundromat's that way."

"Nah," I said. "I'll take you to the one on Ocean Street. More machines, quality soap in the dispensers, sea breeze outside. It's way better."

She stared at me a moment. "You rate laundromats?"

"Trust me. It's a little farther but you'll never go to another one."

"Okay." She chuckled. "But if my clothes don't come out cleaner, you're making dinner next time."

Next time? She just hinted at another date. Or, at least a more official date. A flash of excitement went through me. "You got it. Toast and cereal okay?

She patted me on the shoulder. "Don't worry, I'll help."

I took the Porsche down Ocean Boulevard at a breezy pace, with the windows down. The cool, salty air felt like mist from heaven after a sweltering day.

Amber closed her eyes and reclined next to me. Her rich,

caramel hair moved playfully about her face in the breeze. Everything was right with the world.

Bright headlights veered from oncoming traffic into my lane. They were headed straight for me. My body snapped out of it's relaxed state and cranked the wheel to the right. Headlights flooded into my window. I braced for impact. The piercing screech of metal and shattered glass rang in my ears as the oncoming car dug into the rear drivers side of the Porsche. The impact spun the car sideways, angling our forward momentum toward oncoming traffic. Everything in my body tensed. I pulled the steering wheel hard to avoid another collision and ended up overcompensating. The Porsche swerved right, the tires sliding out of control. We hammered over the curb with a violent shutter and into the unforgiving concrete of a street lamp.

CHAPTER 12

Everything seemed to move in slow motion for several moments. My head felt like a metal gong that someone had just hit with a mallet. The bright lights of the dashboard streaked across my vision.

A burning odor hung in the air. The airbags had deployed, covering me in a white powder. The spider web cracks of the windshield revealed a devilish puzzle of the hood crumpled against the concrete street lamp. The impact was the worst on the passenger side.

Amber sat motionless beside me. Her eyes were closed, her head leaning back against the head rest. A stream of blood painted red lines from her temple down her neck.

It was like a bad dream in which I was a detached observer unable to fully react to the dark scene around me. I was vaguely aware of arms reaching in and helping me out of the car. Someone led me to the nearby curb where a few people were already gathered. I sat down and, the curb swayed like the hull of a ship. My hands gripped the concrete, waiting for my body to stabilize.

Amber stumbled toward me, the supportive arm of a heavy set older man with a grey beard guiding her to the curb. She held a white handkerchief stained with blood against her forehead.

"Are you okay?" I reached out as the older man lowered her to the curb.

Her eyes were shut tight as if in pain. "I think so."

"That car swerved right into me," I said. "I couldn't avoid it."

She nodded, her eyes still closed.

"You two just take it easy," the old man said. "Ambulance is on it's way."

I felt so guilty watching Amber in pain. It all happened so fast there was no time to react. More than anything else I wanted her to be okay.

My vision righted, and the ground felt solid once more. I took a wary look at the Porsche. The concrete light post stood resolute in the crushed metal folds of the hood. The car that hit us was nowhere in sight.

The high pitched siren and distant flash of red signaled the approach of a police car and an ambulance. Paramedics arrived and checked our vitals, all the while asking us questions, apparently to make sure we didn't pass out on the spot.

After several minutes of medical attention, I was basically given a clean bill of health. Amber was put in one of those puffy, white neck collars and taken into the ambulance to, as they put it, "run additional tests at the hospital to rule out complications." I was sick to my stomach watching the paramedics escort her away instead of me. Even though hitting the other car was unavoidable, I couldn't shake the feeling of guilt.

I followed her up to the ambulance door. "I'll call you later. Make sure everything's okay." It sounded so lame and empty as I heard myself say the words, but it was all I could think of at the moment.

Amber gave a weak smile in return. One of the paramedics motioned me to step back and shut the ambulance door. In a flash of swirling red lights and the shriek of a siren, they took Amber away from me. I stood there watching them leave, feeling totally helpless.

"You the driver?" a voice called behind me.

I turned to find a cop with wire-frame glasses. He held a notepad and pen ready to take down all my info.

"Yeah," I said.

"I'll need your license and registration."

I handed over my license and lead him to the heart-breaking scene of the smashed Porsche. After fishing through the glove box, I found the registration paper.

The cop adjusted his glasses and scanned the registration. "Solastine Callow." He looked up at me. "Family or friend?"

"My boss," I said.

"Ouch." He shook his head.

"Any word on the other car?" I said.

"An eyewitness said it was a grey El Camino. If we spot one with your paint job running down its dented side, we'll have our hit and run."

"Wait..." My mind flashed back to the other night outside The Spinning Parrot. "Last night a grey El Camino tried to run me down on a crosswalk."

The cop paused. "Do you know anyone who owns an El Camino that might want to hurt you?"

"I don't even know anyone who wants an El Camino."

He frowned. "Did you get the license plate?"

"No."

"Well, I'll add it to my notes. Give me a sec. Gotta call this in. You should arrange a ride home." He walked to his car, mumbling cop speak into his radio.

The fact that a grey El Camino came after me twice was a little too coincidental. Was somebody trying to kill me? Other than occasional online arguments, I couldn't think of anyone I'd pissed off that bad.

The mess of laundry that spilled out of Amber's hamper on the back seat was a perfect visual of my life. I leaned in and gathered her things, putting them all back into the hamper. As I stuffed the last pair of ripped jeans inside the basket and pushed the lid as far as it would go, I knew something was off. It took me a moment to realize the problem. A flash of panic hit me as I plunged my arm under both seats, searching. I checked the front seats and even unloaded the hamper again but came up empty.

The package—Solas' package—was gone.

CHAPTER 13

After searching the hamper again and every nook of the car and the surrounding street, I gave up. Someone had taken the package. All I could see were mounting dollar signs and lifelong debt payments. I stood by the crumpled Porsche, trying to take deep breaths to calm the rising panic.

The cop strolled up. "I notified the owner. She's having it towed. Said she'd contact you soon."

"That should be fun." My stress level was high enough that I was actually speaking my thoughts.

The cop grinned. "I feel for ya buddy. You should call someone, get a ride home."

I grabbed Amber's hamper from the back seat. I didn't want to send her to the hospital and lose all her clothes in the same night. For a moment I considered calling Steve. I imagined the grief he'd give me when he found out about the crashed Porsche and lost package, so I requested an Uber driver instead.

A few minutes later a mustard-colored economy car

picked me up. The driver was a middle-aged Indian man with a wild salt and pepper goatee. As he drove me home and we shared small talk, I kept waiting for his eyes to glow green and turn into my crazy angel. But it never happened.

He dropped me off in front of my apartment and gave a tap of his horn on the way out. I felt very alone at that moment.

Where was Finch? For once I wished he would appear and bug me some more. There was a thick pocket of stress lodged somewhere between my heart and stomach. My loaner Porsche was wrecked and the mystery package was gone. Would Solas expect me to pay for it? If it was anything of value, I'd probably be working for her for free for the next year.

Even worse, I'd just put the girl I was falling for in the hospital. It's not the type of first date story she'd want to tell people about. Plus, once her friends heard my bio—an unemployed comic book artist who lives in an oven temperature, stink-hole apartment—they'd tell her the accident was a sign, and off to Heath's arms she'd go.

Carrying the load of unwashed laundry, I trudged up the stairs to my place and froze in the hallway. The front door of my apartment was open. I set Amber's hamper down in the hall. My hand shot into my pocket and instinctively grabbed my keys. One of these days I had to invest in a real knife.

There was a shuffling sound inside. Something or someone was moving around in my apartment. I crept to the threshold. My imagination conjured up a host of dark shadows moving through the rooms and hiding behind furniture.

A sudden anger that I was afraid of my own home rose inside me. With that, I threw caution to the wind and stepped through the doorway. A bloated figure hunched near the wall. I flinched, my body tensing for the next action.

Relief hit me when I realized it was just the apartment super leaning over the wall heater.

"Hey, Craig." The super saluted me with a wrench.

I let out a long breath. "It's *Chris*."

"Chris. Sorry. I don't see your name much. I usually get the rent checks from Steve." A grin animated the pudgy jowls under his greasy, brown hair.

I only saw him about once a month, but he never missed an opportunity to get a dig in about rent money. Even though Steve signed our late rent checks, somehow the super knew the overdue payment was my fault.

The super clinked his wrench on the metal wall heater. "I have to order a new part for the full repair, but I made a temporary fix."

I took tentative steps into the apartment. It wasn't quite sauna level anymore but far from cool. "It's still pretty hot in here."

He nodded. "Like I said, temporary fix." He put the wrench on his tool belt and made for the door. "Just open all the windows. Should be fine until the right part comes in."

"How long will that be?"

He barely looked back as he exited. "Just a day or two. Say hi to Steve for me." His carefree whistle echoed down the hallway as he left.

I cursed him under my breath and retrieved Amber's clothes from the hall. Soon I had every window opened in the apartment to counter the stuffy heat. The lazy evening breeze meandered in like sap out of a tree.

Sweat beaded on my forehead, and pronounced pit stains gave my Iron Man shirt a two-toned appearance. It was 9:00 at night, and I was sweating. I made a vow to never again live in a place without an air conditioner.

I opened the freezer door and stuck my head in among the ice trays for a few minutes. It helped a little, so I waited for the heat to return in full force, then tried it again. This time I felt a little dizzy. I was no doctor, but leaving my body in the desert while my head vacationed in Alaska was probably a recipe for a hospital visit.

The thought of the hospital brought me right back to Amber. I couldn't help feeling it was my fault she was injured. My lack of medical training left no frame of reference to understand how she was doing. Going to the hospital for follow-up tests could mean nothing or the worst.

It was weird to be so concerned about someone I'd just started to get to know, but she was special. We had an amazing connection. It was the kind of relationship I'd been longing for. Hopefully she felt the same ... provided I didn't send her into the ER for emergency surgery. I decided to stop worrying and call her directly.

"Hello?" Her voice sounded a little drowsy.

"Hey, it's Chris. How are you?"

"Oh, I'm okay. Just tired," she said. "I passed all their tests. I'm headed home."

The tense feeling in my neck and shoulders relaxed a little. "That's great. I'm really sorry, Amber. That car came right at me."

"I know. It's not your fault. Don't worry, I'll be fine. By the way, Heath says hi."

I was silent for a moment. "Heath? He's there?"

"Yeah. He heard I got into an accident and stopped by the hospital to make sure I was okay."

"Oh." A thought flashed through my mind of smashing an acoustic guitar over Heath's head. For some reason he really brought out the violent side of my imagination. "Well, that was ... nice of him."

"Yeah, he's a sweetie," she said. "Listen, I'm going to my mom's. She's all freaked out and wants to watch me all night or something."

"Right." I paused. "That's cool." Not being able to see her tonight after what happened left a pit in my stomach.

"Did the super ever show up?" she asked.

"Yeah, but he just put a bandaid on the problem. Our apartment is still five thousand degrees."

She laughed. It felt really good to hear her laugh again.

"Okay, well, I guess I'll see you tomorrow at Caring Tables."

"For sure. See you at lunch."

I clicked off, the mantle of defeat settling heavy across my shoulders. I figured the best way to get my mind off things was to stay busy.

I went to my computer. When it blinked to life, I searched the internet for cheap ways to cool down your place. Thankfully, I found what I needed. After several attempts, the combined efforts of three different DIY cooling techniques involving mounds of ice cubes and fans managed to bring the temperature down by about one degree.

By midnight, I was in my underwear, lying on top of my bed. Steve never came home. He probably took the smarter path and stayed with family or friends who owned air conditioners.

Sleep didn't come easy, but after about an hour in a heat-induced haze, I faded off toward dreamland. Right before I drifted to sleep, I could've sworn a shadow moved in the corner of my room.

CHAPTER 14

◆

Novel Crepes on Second Street wasn't my typical breakfast stop. In fact, I couldn't remember the last time I had a crepe. It seemed like a rich man's pancake.

After a broken, sweaty night's sleep, another Uber ride dropped me in front of the restaurant and took more of my dwindling money. My unemployed funds were growing ever thinner. It was time to bug Steve for more rides.

The crepe restaurant was decked out in plum and crimson tones. Dark wood booths tucked diners into cozy breakfast nooks. Since I was ten minutes late, it was no surprise Solas was already seated at a booth up front, her coffee cup half empty.

She gave a tight smile at my arrival and stood. Her off-white pant suit and her hair pulled back made breakfast feel more like a job interview.

I'd rehearsed a few different ways to explain the car accident and lost package. In the end, it seemed better to play dumb and fake shell shock from the crash.

I moved toward her with a subtle limp. "Morning. Sorry I'm late. Guess I'm still a little out of it."

Solas gave me a warm embrace followed by an unexpected kiss that lasted longer than just a friendly greeting. Only yesterday I'd welcomed her affections. Now I felt a tinge of guilt. Even though I hadn't even taken Amber on an official date, my heart was already there.

It seemed a little insane to want to tell the blonde supermodel in front of me that I didn't want to kiss her anymore, but it had to be done. The future me would probably look back on this decision and hate the present me, but it was necessary. I'd just have to find a way to tell her after I ironed out the whole smashed car and lost package problem.

Solas leaned back and smiled. "I'm glad you're okay. Did the doctor check you out?"

"Um, yeah. I mean, the paramedic guy did."

"What did he say about your leg?" She said.

"Huh?"

"You were limping."

"Oh." I forgot all about my fake injury."I think it's just a sprain or something. I'm fine."

She looked down at my hands. "Where's the package?"

"Right ... The package." This is where she might start yelling. "I left it in the car. Did the police find it?"

She stared at me a moment. "No. Chris, that was very important."

"I know. I'm really sorry. Will your car insurance cover it?"

She let out a stressful-sounding exhale. "No."

Solas slumped down in the booth and started rapid fire texting. I waited a few moments not sure if I should sit down or just keep my mouth shut a while.

She finished texting and looked up at me. "That was an expensive package. I really wish you would have brought it to me last night like I asked."

I joined her in the booth. "I know. I'm sorry, but listen, I don't know what's going on. That warehouse where I picked it up was really sketchy. Did you know the same thug that did this to me"—I pointed to my cheekbone which had begun to turn an unsightly color of purple—"was working on electronics there. Probably stolen electronics. Is that what I'm delivering?"

"Stolen?" Her eyes narrowed. "You think I'm dealing with stolen goods?"

I put up my hands. "Look, it's none of my business, I just don't want to be involved in it."

She shook her head. "Chris, refurbished electronics is a profitable business. There's no need to deal in stolen merchandise. There's more money running a legitimate company with the right team of legal people behind you."

"What about that thug?" I said. "They said his name was Trench."

"That warehouse is a rehabilitation work center," she said. "One of my charities helps ex-cons learn technical trade skills so they can integrate back into society. I don't know anyone named Trench, but I'll put in a call. He shouldn't be there if he's still committing crimes."

"Oh ... Okay." I ran through the list of objections I'd been worried about. It seemed as if she'd answered them all.

She reached across the table and put her hand on mine. "I'm glad I could address your concerns. I want you to be comfortable with this job."

"Yeah," I said. "I guess I misjudged things. Sorry again about the car. I hate that I wrecked something that beautiful."

Solas gave my hand a squeeze. "It's okay. You can use the Ferrari for a while."

"Um ... What?"

She pulled out a shiny set of keys and handed them to me. "It's the red 360 Spider just outside."

I took the keys and stared at them for a few moments.

Solas leaned forward. "From now on, I need you to respond to my calls. We have to make up financially for that lost package. I need to rely on you. I need to be your first priority. Can you commit to that?"

I nodded, unable to look away from the shiny keys.

"Great." She smiled. "I'm going to use the ladies room. Breakfast should be here soon. I took the liberty of ordering." She got up and headed for the bathroom.

I leaned out of the booth and looked toward the street. Right out front a cherry red Ferrari waited for me, sunlight gleaming off it's aerodynamic frame.

"This is the greatest job ever," I mumbled to myself.

"Oh? What job would that be?" a familiar voice said.

Finch, clothed in waiter garb and holding two crepe plates, stood before me.

"Finch!" I said. "Where you been?"

"Well, I can't babysit you all day." He set a plate of crepes covered in blueberries and powdered sugar in front of me. "Island of the Blue Dolphins for the gentleman." He set another crepe plate with strawberries across from me. "And The Scarlett Letter for the lady." He brushed off his hands. "Is this for your 'new boss?'" He used air quotes. "My competitor angel?"

"Yeah," I said. "And she's not an angel. Look, is there a way to get a hold of you? I almost died in a car accident last night. I could've really used an angel's help."

"Why do you think you're not in traction right now?"

I paused. "You were there?"

He shook his head. "No, I was busy. But I heard there was intervention. Friends of mine. Not as stylish or personable as me, but still, solid spirits. Forces were after you last night. Things are escalating. We need to ramp up our efforts."

"Someone's after me?" I narrowed my eyes, not liking the thought of being a target of violence, especially coming from supernatural forces. "Who?"

He flipped through his waiter notepad and started reading.

"Initial reports reference low level demons and calloused humans under demonic influence. You know, the usual."

"Is this for real?" I felt angry and terrified at the same time. "Are you messing with me?"

He shook his head. "I told you there was an element of danger."

"Well, call it off." I waved my hands. "I don't want this. Shouldn't they be after a missionary or something?"

He put his hands on his hips. "Oh, man-up, you big baby. This is spiritual warfare. If you quit now, evil wins. Is that what you want?"

"No, but this is crazy. I sent the girl I'm falling for to the hospital last night after almost killing both of us."

"I told you, my friends were on it."

"Where were you? Aren't you supposed to be my guardian angel or something?"

"Trust me," Finch said. "I'm working behind the scenes. There's a lot of pieces to this puzzle." He leaned in confidentially. "If you must know, something's been blocking my efforts. Something big. If you have some habitual sins in your life, now would be a good time to repent. It strengthens the connection. And, if you really want to get serious,"—he pointed to my crepes—"lay off food for a while. A fast can bring laser-like focus on spiritual efforts."

The click of heels against the tile floor signaled Solas's return. She paused, locking eyes with Finch.

"Hello." She gave a polite grin before taking her seat in the booth.

Finch was wide-eyed. His eyes ping-ponged between us. He pointed at her. "*This* is your boss?"

I gave a wary look to Solas. "Yeah."

Finch took a step back, narrowing his eyes at Solas. "So this is where all the spiritual interference is coming from." His voice raised as if accusing someone of a crime.

Customers nearby looked over. A line of concern formed on Solas's forehead. "What's going on? Is this a joke?"

"It's okay." A flush of embarrassment washed through me. "I know him. He's ... eccentric." I turned to Finch. "Calm down, man. You're making a scene."

"I was right, Chris." Finch glared at Solas. "She is an angel—a fallen angel."

CHAPTER 15

Customers near our booth in Novel Crepes whispered to each other and stared, trying to figure out Finch's odd behavior.

"Leave Chris alone." Finch spoke to Solas in elevated dramatics like a prosecutor in a courtroom with damning evidence.

"Chris?" Solas gave me a stern look. "If this is a joke between you and your friend here, I don't appreciate it. I'm about to leave."

"Yes!" Finch pointed at her, his eyes wide with excitement. "Order her to leave like we talked about."

"Knock it off, Finch." I locked eyes with him. "Just go, and we'll talk about it later."

"Oh, you're casting *me* out?" He pointed to himself, eyebrows raised. "That's the thanks I get?"

A middle-aged guy in a button down shirt and slacks stormed out of the back room. He had the wrath of a restaurant manager, disturbed from paperwork, pouring out of him. He stood behind Finch and crossed his arms. "You don't work here. I called the police. Stop harassing the customers and beat it."

A woman in the booth next to us started clapping.

My head was spinning. Finch was freaking me out. I glanced over at Solas. She looked thoroughly human ... and perfect. He had to be off on this one. I started doubting everything. Maybe he wasn't an angel after all. Maybe he was just an off-balanced hypnotist like Steve thought.

Finch's jaw went tight. "Fine." He looked at me as he headed for the door. "I can't fight your free will. You're on your own."

The manager shadowed him and shut the door as he left. He turned. "Sorry folks. Dessert is on the house."

More clapping from the woman next to us.

I turned to Solas. "I'm so sorry. He's really into spiritual stuff. Very active imagination."

Her eyes teared up, and she looked away. "I don't like being spoken to in that way, Chris. I'm very upset right now."

The manager came to our booth. "Everyone okay? I apologize. He must've stolen one of our uniforms."

"We're fine," I said. "No big deal."

"Breakfast is on us," he said. "Order whatever you like."

"I need this to go." Solas pointed at her crepes. "I can't eat after that."

The manager gave a slight bow. "I understand." He signaled a waitress nearby. "Nicole, can you wrap this up for her?"

The waitress nodded and whipped Solas's food off to the kitchen.

"Please come back another time," the manager said. "Your next meal is on me." He smiled and made his way to Ms. Claps-a-Lot in the next booth.

"So, that was a friend of yours that yelled at me?" Solas pulled a tissue from her purse and dabbed at her eyes.

"Well, *friend* is a strong word."

She sniffed. "My father spoke to me like that. Authoritative, condemning ... it was traumatic."

"I really don't know Finch that well," I said. "He's a little off. It'll never happen again."

Solas let out a long breath. "Well, I have to go."

"You sure?" I felt like the whole thing was my fault. "Why don't you stay and eat. It'll make you feel better."

She shook her head. "I have work to do. It's going to be a busy day. I'll text you for deliveries. We need to make up for that package."

I held up my phone. "I'll be ready."

As the waitress returned with the wrapped breakfast, Solas stood and walked out the door. A black limousine pulled up to the curb and let her in. As the limo drove away, I noticed she hadn't taken her crepes.

The Ferrari Spider on city streets was like driving a race car on a kiddie park motorway. It seemed as if the typical roads just couldn't contain it. It wanted out. I needed a helmet and gloves to justify driving such a fine piece of machinery. Still, even driving this dream car on common streets was a beautiful experience.

I took the Ferrari toward the coastline. Soon I was cruising down Ocean Boulevard, blasting the radio and trying to get my mind off things. My thoughts drifted between song lyrics and simpler times. I sat back in the perfectly designed racing seat and relaxed to the visual rhythm of the palm trees gliding by.

After the morning, and half the gas tank, was spent, I decided to head back to reality. As fun as pretending to be a race car driver was, I couldn't avoid my troubled thoughts. I didn't know how to process Finch's outburst. I'd been slowly buying into the angel reality, but now I didn't know what to think. Supernatural involvement in my life was so divorced from the reality I knew. Maybe I needed to visit a pastor for guidance. He'd probably think I was crazy. There was really only one person I could hit with this level of weird.

I drove back to my apartment and found Steve painting in the front room. All the windows were open and fans were placed at strategic corners to counter the relentless assault of the broken heater. The weak breeze and fans were losing the battle: the apartment still felt like a sauna.

Steve was busy on a new art piece, almost as bleak as the last one. A dark figure ran through a ruined city scape. A frayed strand of white rope languished on a hillside behind him.

"More happy art?" I said.

He barely cracked a grin, his paintbrush adding dark strokes. "I paint what I feel around me. It's emotional honesty."

"Just be glad you didn't sleep here last night. You'd be painting the fires of hell."

He stopped painting and turned to me. "You actually slept here?"

"It was part sleeping, part slow roasting."

"Brutal. The super called me. Said the part should come in today."

"He calls you directly?"

Steve nodded and went back to painting.

I gave a nervous clearing of my throat. "Can I talk to you?"

He sighed. "More angels and supermodels?"

"Maybe."

"Make it quick. I'm totally in the zone right now. Inspiration is flowing."

There was no normal way to address the weirdness, so I just let it out. "What would you say if my angel met the woman I'm working for and called her a fallen angel. Which, I guess, is a demon, right?"

He put down his brush. "Swear to me right now you're not using."

I put up my hands. "Dude, I'm clean. You know I've never done drugs in my life."

"You smoked out with Becky Semoure."

"I took one puff." I frowned. "Her blue eyes hypnotized me."

He pursed his lips and nodded a few times. "I don't know what to say. You seem crazy lately."

"My life is crazy. That's why I'm asking for help."

"Maybe you just need some distance from stressful stuff," he said. "You need to unplug. Go somewhere peaceful for a while."

"I can't. I told Amber I'd help at Caring Tables for lunch."

"That's perfect. When I was stuck on a painting last week, I volunteered at the food bank and bam, suddenly I knew just how to finish it."

I gave him a blank stare. "So, volunteering is supposed to solve my personal problems?"

"It gives you a new perspective. Takes your mind off yourself for awhile. Clears out the clutter." He turned back to his painting. "Call me when you're done. We'll hang and talk it out."

How filling up plates of food for the homeless would keep angels, fallen or not, from complicating my life was beyond me. Steve sure seemed confident about the whole idea. Who knew? Maybe it would help.

"Okay," I said. "But I need a favor."

He frowned. "What?"

"Can I borrow your car?"

"Let me guess, you don't want to take the Porsche over there."

Getting into the whole smashed Porsche and new Ferrari story was just too much at the moment.

"Something like that," I said.

He fished keys out of his pocket and threw them to me. "Not a scratch."

I grabbed an energy drink and a couple granola bars on the way out, just in case the soup kitchen was serving up something funky. Steve's battered old econo car was a far cry from the Ferrari. Still, he owned one and I didn't, so it was hard to complain. I pulled up to Caring Tables just before 12:30 and headed inside.

Amber was in her apron, wiping off one of the tables. Unfortunately, Heath was right next to her, filling the salt shaker. He said something, and she broke out in a laugh. Her rich brown eyes sparkled, and her perfect smile was aimed right at him. It was as if I'd shown up late for a race, and the winner had already been crowned.

CHAPTER 16

What a bad start to my volunteering day. Anyone could see Amber and Heath had well-established chemistry. Relationship history was a tough mountain to overcome. He already knew all the best pathways and had a team of Sherpas shouldering his pack while I was scaling a cliff face in the dark. Still, I wasn't ready to give up until Amber turned me away or put me in the dreaded friend zone.

I headed straight for Amber, hoping to break Man Bun's spell on her. Her face lit up as our eyes met. Having someone as amazing as Amber happy to see me woke an excitement deep inside that I hadn't felt since high school.

She hurried over and gave me a hug. "Hey, Chris."

"Hi." I noticed a butterfly bandage at the corner of her forehead. "How you feeling?"

"Oh, I'm fine." She waved me off like I was some protective parent. "Just a little scratch." She motioned to her forehead. "Was your boss mad about the car?"

"Surprisingly, no. She's got insurance. Plus she's loaded, so I don't think it was a huge deal."

"In that case, see if she donates to charity. This place needs help."

Heath slid up next to us. "Hey, bro. Heard about the accident. Be careful out there, man."

"Yeah." I said. "Crazy drivers. What can you do?"

"Gotta drive defensive." He put his hands out as if gripping a steering wheel at nine and three o' clock. "Especially in a squirrelly sports car."

My jaw clenched reflexively. Was he throwing fault for the accident at me?

"Nothing I could do, bro." I purposely threw his favorite 'bro' term back in his face. "The car came right into my lane."

He patted my shoulder, his blue eyes pools of sincerity. "I'm just glad you two are okay."

He was like a conversation assassin. Slipping in for an sly accusation, then backing out again with warmth and concern. I had to get rid of him.

"No guitar today?" I said. "Music would be great with lunch."

"Really?" He looked toward the corner of the room where his guitar lay propped on a stand like a dog begging for a walk. "I mean, I don't want to bail on the lunch line."

"Don't worry." I slapped him on the shoulder. "I'll pick up the slack. What this place needs is some tunes."

He turned to Amber, his brows raised.

She gave a nod. "It was nice yesterday."

"All right." He started removing his apron. "Maybe just a song or two."

"Just keep it chill," I said. "Don't want to make it into a concert or anything."

He pointed at me and grinned. "I hear you."

Heath strode into the tractor-beam pull of musician and awaiting guitar.

Amber turned to me. "So, you like Heath's music, huh?"

I shrugged. "Background music is always good when you're eating."

Amber looked at me, a skeptical sort of squint in her eye.

"Mm. Well, you ready for the serving line?"

"You bet." I shut off the ringer on my phone. This was quality time with Amber, and I didn't want crazy texts from Finch or demanding deliveries from Solas getting in the way. A tinge of guilt nagged at my thoughts. I'd promised Solas only this morning I'd be on constant call. I hesitated a moment.

"Everything okay?" Amber said.

"Yeah. Of, course." I smiled at my own paranoia and stuffed the phone back in my pocket. After all, every job has a lunch break. It's not like I was getting called in for emergency surgery or anything.

As the lunch line came on, I stood shoulder to shoulder with Amber dishing out string beans, coleslaw, and chicken nuggets. Once again I was disappointed with the lack of soup in this soup kitchen.

Amber glanced over at me, her experienced hands dishing out servings of coleslaw with assembly-line efficiency. "I forgot to ask about your graphic novel pitch. How'd your meeting go yesterday?"

"Good, I think." My serving spoon wasn't cooperating with the string beans. By the time I lifted a full scoop to the plate, most had rolled back into the metal tray. I had to go back for a second scoop for each plate. I was definitely the bottleneck of the line. "The woman I pitched to liked it. She's got industry connections. She's actually the one who offered me the new job."

"The one with the Porsche?" Amber said. "The delivery job?"

"Yep. Pays pretty great too."

Amber paused a moment. "Is she family?"

"No, I just met her."

"Hm." Her face had a studied look.

"What?" I said.

"Seems like a lot to do for someone she just met. What are you delivering exactly?"

"I think it's just refurbished electronics and stuff."

Amber nodded. "Sounds too good to be true. There's big money floating behind illegal deliveries around here. Not saying that's what you're doing, but you better make sure."

"Ain't that the truth." A homeless lady in a purple jogging suit stopped in front of us. "Listen to her." She looked at me while pointing at Amber. "She knows."

"Um, okay," I said.

Jogging suit lady gave a pronounced nod and moved on.

We spent the next hour talking and joking around as we served up lunch. It was like hanging out with a good friend at summer camp. I couldn't remember the last time I had such a great connection with a woman.

The lunch line eventually died down, and Heath joined us at the counter. I lost track of how many songs he'd ended up playing while I spent one-on-one time with Amber. It was a beautiful turn of events.

"Sorry I stuck you guys with the rush." Heath tied on his apron. "Got caught up with the music."

"No worries," I said. "If you grab dishes, we'll call it even."

His face tightened, and he gave a forced grin.

"You sounded great," Amber said. "I heard some new ones."

"Yeah," he gave a wistful look skyward. "Wrote a ton in Costa Rica. Easier to write in a chill spot like that."

"Cool." Amber smiled and grabbed a plate. "Well, all I had for breakfast was toast and coffee. Smelling all this food without eating is torture." She started loading up her own plate.

"All right." Heath grabbed my shoulder. "Guess we'll handle any stragglers that come through, right Chris?"

"Actually." I grabbed a plate and started filling up. "I'm pretty hungry, too. I need to break for lunch."

From the corner of my eye I caught Heath frowning. Obviously I was irritating him. Whether it was because of Amber or my occasionally annoying personality, it was hard to tell. Either way, what could I do? I was falling hard for Amber, and if he was trying to rekindle some old flame, I wasn't just going to sit back and let that happen. From what she told me about their past, he wasn't the right guy for her. She deserved someone who wasn't led by the nose with the latest adrenaline rush.

I finished filling my plate and followed Amber to a table where two guys in jeans and T-shirts were just finishing their lunch. The experience of working the lunch counter introduced me to a broad spectrum of homeless. Aside from those with grungy brown clothes in desperate need of a bath—the ones I would've typically pegged as homeless—there were quite a few like the two guys at the table. People who looked like anyone else. I would've passed them on the street without ever realizing they had to find lodging at some shelter or a friend's house.

"Hey guys." Amber greeted them as she took a seat at the table.

"Amber," they said, practically in unison.

"Chris, this is Carl and Eddie." She motioned to them.

"Hey." I shook their hands and took a seat next to Amber.

"Newbie, huh?" Carl said. He looked to be in his late thirties, with dusty brown hair, a goatee, and a receding hairline.

"Yeah," I said.

Eddie looked a few years younger than Carl. He was clean shaven with shoulder length black hair smoothed back like a faux mullet. He leaned back, studying me for a moment. "I'm guessing seminary student earning credits."

Carl grinned. "Na. Struggling actor up for a homeless role. He's getting into character."

Eddie pointed at him. "Bingo."

I laughed. These guys were awesome. "Not even close."

"All right, hold on, don't tell me." Eddie examined my clothes as if they were hidden clues. "Unemployed writer looking for inspiration."

I shook my head.

Carl slapped him on the shoulder. "Maybe we should just go with the obvious." He motioned to me and Amber. "Volunteer with ulterior motives."

Eddie high-fived him. "Nailed it."

"Carl!" Amber playfully scolded him.

No use denying the truth. "Guilty." I put up my hands in surrender. "But I gotta say, this place is growing on me."

"Mm-hm." Carl nudged Eddie like he wasn't buying it.

"No, really." I said. "I kinda feel like I've missed out. I'll definitely be back."

Eddie nodded. "Well, if you really want to sink your teeth into things, why don't you talk to Beck over there." He motioned to a table in the corner. An old, skinny guy in a shabby brown trench coat and wiry grey hair sat by himself.

"Yeah," Carl said. "He could really use a friend."

"Oh, stop it," Amber said. "You guys are punks."

"No, it's okay." I stood. "Why not?"

Amber grabbed my hand. "Chris, they're messing with you."

"All the more reason to do it." I walked over to the homeless guy they called Beck. He was seated by himself, staring off into space. A chicken nugget impaled on his fork remained poised in front of him as if he forgot it was there.

I couldn't deny the positive jolt this place had given me. It was like every minute meant something, like I was contributing to a larger effort. Coming here to be close to Amber got me here, but it had become something more. Something I wanted to be a part of. The way I looked at it, I wanted to see every part of it, even this odd loner in the corner.

"Hi. Beck, right?" I looked down at him. "Mind if I sit here?"

Without breaking his statue-like position, he let his eyes slide over to me. "You CIA?"

"Nope." I smiled. "Civilian."

His eyes shifted away. "Only CIA allowed."

"Oh." I searched for another angle. "How 'bout those chicken nuggets? Next time I'm bringing barbecue sauce. Beats ketchup, right?"

He turned his head to me. "You know what they put in these? Junk!"

I nodded. "Probably. Tastes pretty good though."

"It's synthetic." He shook the nugget on his fork at me. "Grown in a lab. And we're the rats." He shook the nugget again. "Lab rats."

Heath's voice called out from the lunch counter. "Got pudding for dessert. First come, first served."

Beck stood and pointed at me. "Don't touch my nuggets." He turned and headed for the lunch line.

When I got back to Amber, Carl and Eddie were stifling laughter like a couple of high school kids.

"How'd it go." Eddie grinned and elbowed Carl.

"Well, I don't want my chicken anymore," I said.

Carl raised his hand. "Dibs."

"How old are you two?" Amber shook her head. "Finish your lunch with us, Chris."

I sat and started in on the coleslaw.

"Yep, there's all kinds here," Carl said. "Users, crazies, and then there's the rest of us, just trying to turn things around."

"Beck's not crazy," Amber said.

"Oh yeah?" Carl said. "Just yesterday he claimed he ate lunch with an angel named Finchelus."

I winced.

"Oh, stop it." Amber slapped his arm. "He just needs psychiatric help. If we ever get enough funding, we can add that to our services."

Eddie shrugged. "Either way, we're on our way out of this system." He looked at me. "Carl and I used to work the oil platforms offshore. Layoffs last year sent us spiraling. Lost my place, my truck, even my girl bailed on me. And Carl, well, Carl can't get a girl, whether he's employed or not."

Carl punched him. "Shut the hell up."

"Anyway," Eddie chuckled. "Things are looking up. I snagged a job at Reeds Supply down the street. Pulled some strings and got Carl hired on last week."

Carl dropped his fork with a sigh. "Third time you brought that up today. You'd think you gave me a kidney."

Eddie continued. "It's just part time, but it was enough to pool our money and get an apartment nearby."

Amber motioned to them. "See? Getting people back on their feet. This is what it's all about."

"That's awesome," I said.

"Yeah," Carl said. "We're moving in tonight. It's not the best apartment, but it'll do for now."

"It's a rat hole," Eddie said. "And their laundry room has a busted washer."

"Don't worry," Amber said. "The super said he'd fix it soon."

"Wait." I turned to Amber. "They're moving into our apartment complex?"

She nodded. "I vouched for them."

"Oh." Eddie shared a guilty look with Carl. "Just kidding about the rat hole thing. It's not such a bad place."

"Yeah," Carl forced a smile. "It's kinda clean."

"Forget it," I waved them off. "I know it's bad. It's all I can afford."

"I heard that," Eddie stood. "Well, I'm going for pudding."

"Yep." Carl followed Eddie to the lunch line.

When it got right down to it, I was probably only a few steps away from this place myself. I turned back to Amber and found her smiling at me.

"What?" I said.

"So, you volunteered with ulterior motives, huh?"

"Big surprise?"

"Shocker," she grinned. "I have to admit, when I meet a cute guy, this place is a good test to see if they're a giver or a taker. Or, to put it in your sci-fi terms, it's like a time machine to check the future of a relationship."

She was learning my language. It had to be love.

"You know," I said. "There's lots of different ways to give."

"Of course. This is just one test."

"And if I made you dinner tonight, that could be another test?"

She smiled. "Now you're getting it. But I can't tonight. Got another shift at the diner."

"Oh, okay."

"She checked her phone. But I don't have to leave for another twenty minutes. You can help me with dishes in the back if you want," she said.

"Another test?"

"Maybe." She grabbed her tray and stood.

"Say no more." Even though I'd cornered Heath into dishwashing duty, which would have been perfect justice since he bailed on me yesterday, a chance for more time with Amber was worth a small loss. I followed her to the large metal sinks in the back where stacks of dishes awaited.

The next twenty minutes flew by. Hanging out with Amber even made dishwashing enjoyable. When she had to leave, we hugged goodbye, and she gave me a quick kiss on the cheek. Things were definitely moving in a good direction. Driving home, I was on cloud nine. Steve was right, the soup kitchen did wonders for my state of mind. It wasn't just my growing connection with Amber, as awesome as that was, I enjoyed working at Caring Tables. I was actually looking forward to going back the next day.

Right as I pulled up to my apartment I realized my ringer was still off. I checked my phone. Five missed calls. All from Solas. An anxiety-driven pressure formed in my temples.

CHAPTER 17

Facing the wrath of five missed calls from Solas was a grim prospect. Good thing this assistant job paid well. I took a deep breath and dialed her number.

"Chris, I've been trying to get a hold of you." She didn't sound happy.

"Sorry. I took a lunch break."

"There's plenty of time for breaks between deliveries. You missed an important one today. I need a quick response on these. I took a big hit on that package you lost yesterday. Not to mention the damage done to the Porsche. In light of all that, I really don't think I'm asking for too much here, Chris."

"You're right. Sorry. I'll stay connected."

"Good. Tomorrow morning I have an urgent pickup. Nine o' clock in Naples. I'll text you the address."

"No problem," I said. "I'll be there."

"Please do. And make sure you're on time."

The connection clicked off. This job was giving me a

nagging sense of claustrophobia. Maybe the crazy things Finch said about Solas were just getting under my skin.

When I thought about it, I really didn't have much to complain about. She was beautiful, rich, and connected. She handed me an easy job with company cars to die for. She offered to help get my graphic novel published. More importantly, my funds were nearly depleted. Without this job I'd be stuck eating synthetic chicken nuggets with Beck. I shook off the worry and headed inside.

I opened the door to our apartment only to be greeted with a stifling heat wave. Steve was heading into the living room carrying a packed duffle bag. Beads of sweat covered his face and his white T-shirt was marked with giant pit stains.

"He still hasn't fixed this?" I said.

"I called the super an hour ago," Steve said. "He said he had to order a special part. Should come in tomorrow."

"Special part? All these apartments have the same heater. Shouldn't he have this stuff on hand?"

Steve shrugged. "All I know is, I ain't sleeping in this oven. I'm headed for my grandma's place."

A sweaty memory of my horrible sleep last night rushed back to me. "Can I come?"

Steve frowned. "You'll crowd me on the fold out."

"I'll sleep on the floor."

"Yeah, right."

I held up my hand. "Promise."

He paused for a moment, taking a deep breath. "Fine. Get your stuff."

In a matter of minutes I had my clothes for the next day jammed into a backpack. I grabbed a few comics and the latest edition of *Car and Driver* magazine and stuffed them in my messenger bag in the highly likely event there was nothing to do at Steve's Grandma's.

Back in the living room, Steve just finished a phone call.

"That was grandma," Steve said. "She said you can come, but it's lights out at nine."

"Jeez, what a tyrant."

He glared at me.

"Dude, I'm kidding. I love your grandma." I patted my backpack. "I'm ready to go."

Steve hoisted his duffle bag over his shoulder. "I have to stop by the art store and get some supplies."

"Okay, you ready for a surprise?" I jingled my car keys in front of him.

"We're taking the Porsche?"

"Better. Look closer."

He leaned forward to inspect the keychain. "Ferrari? What happened to the Porsche?"

"Call it an upgrade."

Steve shook his head and started for the door. "Okay, but if a cop pulls us over, I don't know anything about it."

The Ferrari wove through the Long Beach traffic like a speed bike in a land of scooters. I felt free and alive. Steve seemed annoyed.

"Don't wrap us around a tree," he said. "I've got a painting career ahead of me."

"Relax." I chirped the tires around a turn. "This will give you inspiration."

Steve pointed. "There's the art store. Don't smash into it."

I swerved into the store's parking lot, the car's tires gripping the road like they had claws. I tucked the Ferrari into a spot right in front of the store where I could keep an eye on it.

"Hey, they're hiring." Steve motioned to a place called Craig's Comic Cave next to the art store. A help wanted sign hung in the window.

"Pshh, I want to make comics not sell them."

"Yeah, but you'd be in the thick of the market." Steve said. "I worked at the art store last summer. Made some great contacts."

I scanned the glossy superhero posters blanketing the windows of the comic store. Epic battles and heroic poses trumpeted the dynamic adventures that awaited in the stories on the shelves within. I had to admit, it was pretty inviting.

"Looks cool," I said. "But I already have a job."

"Selling comics is better than selling cocaine."

"It's not cocaine, it's electronics!"

He opened the car door and got out. "If you say so."

Steve strode into the art store without looking back. My fingers drummed against the sleek steering wheel, contemplating my next move. I sighed and headed into Craig's Comic Cave.

Most comic book stores were pretty interchangeable. In fact, you could argue old-school music stores used the same template. These just took the rows and shelves of CDs and replaced them with comic books, then replaced the band posters on the walls with superheroes, and they'd made the switch.

Craig's Comic Cave followed the standard comic store format with the awe inspiring exception of one half wall with mounted replicas of classic superhero and sci-fi weaponry such as Thor's Hammer, Captain America's shield, a few space blasters, and assorted medieval swords. Whoever ran the store was a true fan and collector of classic geekdom.

As I entered, there was an electronic sound that matched the effect of doors opening on the Enterprise.

"Hey." A stout guy with a mop of curly, black hair and a T-shirt that read, "Han Shot First," stocked the new release wall, but glanced over when I entered.

I noticed a replica of Chewbacca's weapon mounted next to a broadsword. "Is that a bow caster?"

"Good eye, my friend." The stout guy set a stack of comics down and turned to me. He looked to be in his early forties with a weary expression that suggested I was already wasting his time. "You buying or browsing?"

"Saw your sign." I motioned to the help wanted sign. "You have any applications?"

"Hm." He leaned over the counter of comics, squinting as if sizing me up. "You know comics?"

"Yep. I'm a fan. I even write them."

He smirked. "Don't we all. Tell you what, answer three questions and you got the job."

"Just three?"

He nodded. "Who was the first superhero to wear a standard costume. You know, spandex style with a mask."

I raised a brow. "Comic trivia? This is the hiring process?"

"You gotta have geek cred in my store. You want the job or not?"

My mind spun through it's dusty storehouse of useless knowledge. "The Phantom?"

"Lucky guess." He straightened as if annoyed by my correct answer. "Okay, how 'bout this one: what hot super chick grew up on Tamaran?"

"Wait, I know this ... Starfire."

His nose crinkled like there was a foul smell. "Took you too long. Passing grade. That's two for two. What's the best-selling comic of all time?"

That one I knew. "X-Men number one."

He nodded. "You ever been to Comic-Con?"

"That's four questions. You said three."

He sighed, waiting for my response.

"Yes, I've been to Comic-Con. Twice."

"Okay. Adequate. The loser you'll be replacing will be gone by Saturday. Come back next week, and I'll give you the rundown."

"So, that's it? I'm hired?"
"You do drugs?"
"No."
"Pot?"
"Isn't that a drug?"
He spread out his hands. "The stoner I just fired said it doesn't count so I gotta ask."
"No pot."
"Good. What's your name?"
"Chris. Chris Loury."
He pointed to himself. "Craig. This is my store. My rules. I pay minimum wage plus two free comics a week."
I nodded. "Fair enough."
He gave me a thumbs up. "Okay, you're in. Come back next week."
"Thanks. See you then." I left the store feeling like that was the best, most straightforward interview process ever.
Next door I found Steve pouring over palette knives.
"Hey," Steve said. "Did you go over there?"
"Yeah."
His brow raised. "And?"
I spread my arms wide. "He saw the skills. I'm hired."
"Serious? No application or anything?"
"What can I say? I'm on a roll lately."
Steve nodded. "Great. Now you can ditch the illegal deliveries."
"Not yet. Maybe I can juggle both."
He shook his head and went back to shopping. "Your funeral."
The next forty minutes passed slowly. Going to the art supply store with Steve was like going antiquing with a retired couple. I grabbed a new art pad and was done in about five minutes. Steve had another approach. To him, an art store was Disneyland in slow motion. He poured over every brush and

canvas. I was tempted to go back to the comic store, but after my triumphant visit, I didn't want to ruin things.

After what felt like ten hours, Steve finally got the supplies he needed and we were back in the Ferrari.

"So, what's grandma got going for dinner?" I said.

"She's not making Kung Pao chicken again," Steve said.

"Oh man, why? Did you ask her? Did you tell her how much I liked it last time?"

"No, she's already letting us stay over. I'm not gonna ask for more favors."

"Maybe she likes making it for guests."

"It's too much work. I told her mac and cheese was fine."

"Mac and cheese? I can make that."

"Dude, you're pushing it."

I held up my hand. "Okay, okay. As long as she has air conditioning."

Grandma Lee's home was a two story cracker box wedged tight between similar homes just off Second Street. We rang the doorbell, and she answered instantly as if she'd been waiting on the other side of the door.

"Steve." She clamped onto Steve with her four foot eleven frame and held tight.

"Hi Nai Nai." He hugged her.

She pulled back and gave me a smile. "Hi, Chris. How's the movie theater job going?"

"I got fired," I said.

She gasped "Oh no."

"It's okay. I got a better job. Check out my company car." I motioned to the Ferrari parked on the street.

"Oooh." She smiled at me. "Can you get Steve a job there too?"

"Pass," Steve said.

Inside, the home was neat as a pin. The furniture looked like it was from the seventies yet somehow appeared brand new. Not only did she have air conditioning, but she liked to run it cold. Walking into the house wasn't far from walking into a meat freezer. After the last couple sweaty days, I didn't mind in the least.

She shuffled through the house showing us the latest knick-knacks she'd picked up at local antique stores. Most of them were breath-mint sized metal containers with intricate carvings and inlays. In my imagination, hints of magic residue lingered inside each one.

Dinner was on the table waiting for us even though it was barely five o' clock. The place settings seemed like they were meant for fine cuisine which made the mac-and-cheese entrée completely out of synch.

As I sat down, Grandma Lee patted my shoulder. "I thought you'd ask for my Kung Pao chicken again. You liked it so much last time."

I shot Steve a dark look. "I loved it. Steve thought it would be too much trouble."

"Oh." She waved Steve off. "It's no trouble. I like making it. I don't get as many visitors these days."

I held my hand out to Steve. "There. You see?"

He shook his head. "We didn't want to impose Grandma. Besides, we like mac and cheese, right Chris."

Steve flashed me a serious look.

"Yeah, of course," I said.

"Well, I hope it tastes okay. My doctor said to cut out gluten so this macaroni is made with garbanzo beans. I haven't quite developed a taste for it yet."

Suddenly I wasn't hungry anymore. I grimaced, prodding a few noodles with my fork as if they were dead worms.

"I'm sure it's fine." Steve shoved a forkful in his mouth and started chewing. I noticed the chewing slow down and his facial muscles tighten for a moment. "It's interesting." He gave a tight smile.

"Oh, good," Grandma Lee said. "Well, I'm going to read a little before bed. It's getting late."

I checked my phone. "It's only five."

"I know. It'll be dark soon." She shuffled into the next room.

"Taco Bell drive through?" I whispered.

Steve shook his head. "She made this for us. Either stay and eat, or you can go back to the apartment."

"Fine." I grunted. I tried a forkful. It was somewhere between play dough and algae. "It's gonna be a long night."

By 9:05, per Grandma's request, the lights were off. We had two ankle level night lights that barely kept us from bumping into furniture as we got ready for bed. She put us in the add-on room above the one car garage. Storage boxes lined the walls, making our small space even smaller.

Steve was on the pullout couch, and I was spread out on the floor beside him.

Grandma Lee left me a green loaner sleeping bag lined with red checkered polyester. Once I unzipped it, I was hit with the aroma of an unwashed relic from a 1980's camping trip. "Wow. This bag reeks."

Steve was tucked under a puffy blue and white patchwork quilt on the pullout. The thin iron frame creaked as he tried to make peace with a bar running under his back. "So don't use it."

I was silent for a moment. "Seems like there's a lot of room on the pullout."

"Don't even think about it."

I stared up at the wood-paneled ceiling. I couldn't remember the last time I'd gone to bed at nine o' clock. Chances were, I'd lay awake thinking about demons. I considered grabbing the *Car and Driver* magazine from my messenger bag and reading by phone light.

"Steve?" I said.

There was silence for a few moments followed by a sigh.

"Are you gonna keep me up all night?" Steve said.

"You're usually painting past midnight."

"Different rules at Grandma's house. She's been really supportive of my art. I want to be respectful."

"So, we can't even talk?"

"She's a light sleeper."

"Just one question?"

"One," Steve said.

"Okay, I know you think I'm going through a weird phase, or whatever, with all the supernatural stuff, but as my best friend, deep down, you do believe me, right?"

"Well..." "I believe you're going through something, I'm not sure what. Maybe stress. Maybe bad chemicals got in your food, I don't know."

"No way. If the chemicals were that strong, I'd be acting all crazy."

He chuckled. "Who says you're not?"

"Okay, but remember when we were ten and you thought you saw a spaceship?"

Steve sighed. "You sure like to bring up that story."

"Well, it's an important event. You were all excited about it, and no one believed you. No one, that is, except me."

"Yes, I know. Thank you. The thing is, that actually happened. I saw a ship. It just happened to be a test plane from the military base, not a spaceship."

"But I believed you, didn't I?"

"We were ten. Every plane at night was a possible spaceship. We're adults now. You can't compare that to your angel visions."

"Maybe not, but just consider the possibility for a second. What if the things I'm telling you are all true? What if I'm actually seeing angels and demons and somehow God is giving me a glimpse into the supernatural world?"

Steve let out a long exhale. "If you're for sure on this, and this has nothing to do with the stupid spaceship story. If you're convinced, then as your friend, I'm with you. But you gotta level with me, do you really believe that's what you're seeing?"

I thought for a few moments. "To be honest, I'm not really sure what to believe."

"Well, if you don't believe it, how do you expect me to?"

I couldn't think of anything to say. My head was filled with doubt. It only made sense that he'd be right there with me.

"Good point," I said.

"Maybe you just need a good night's sleep in a house without a broken heater."

"Let's hope so," I said. "All right, no more questions. I'll go to sleep."

"Hallelujah." He turned to his side, the flimsy iron frame of the pullout bed creaking in protest.

My mind was a whirl with the events of the past few days. Some of the biggest highs and lows had occurred within such a short span of time, it was hard to make sense of it all. I closed my eyes and just let my thoughts flow. Apparently I needed the extra sleep because within seconds I was out.

CHAPTER 18

Grandma Lee offered us gluten free scones and lemon tea for breakfast. I must've been starving 'cause it wasn't half bad.

Solas texted me the address for my morning package pickup, and we were off. I dropped Steve back at our apartment, wished him good luck with the heat, and took off to get to my appointment on time.

The Ferrari Spider sped me down Second Street toward Naples Island. Solas needed a package pickup, and I assured her this one would never leave my sight.

The address led me deep within the winding, one way streets of the pricey homes in Naples. Every so often the road would arc over a canal with boat slips that jutted out from the opulent houses. The slips anchored yachts with names like *Blain's Pride* and *Liquid Assets*.

I arrived at a Tuscan-style three story on Sicilian Walk. Thin juniper trees ringed the home like a wall of green spears. The Ferrari wasn't quite as out of place here. The streets were lined with Lexus, Mercedes, and Beemers, looking like shiny trophies decorating the front yards. I grabbed my messenger bag in case the pickup was something big and headed down the front walkway.

The front door of the home was fashioned from dark wood with intricately carved patterns throughout. It was probably the nicest thing I ever knocked on.

A tall guy in a charcoal turtleneck sweater answered. He was trim with that focused, athletic vibe, like he practiced round house kicks on a heavy bag all day.

"Yes?" Turtleneck said.

"I'm picking up a package for Solas," I said.

His brow lowered. "Who?"

"Oh, um. Ms. Callow?"

He nodded. "And you are?"

"Chr– Uh, Harry," I said.

He stepped aside. "Come on in."

The entryway was a stubby arched passage whose sole purpose was to create anticipation for the swanky space beyond. Terracotta tiles ushered me into a rustic, sun-drenched main room with a vaulted ceiling. Textured walls, rich murals, and iron accents all contributed to a plush lounging area for the rich and exotic.

An overweight guy with a crew cut and Hawaiian shirt glanced up at our arrival. He was lounging on a cushy chaise lounge, tapping away on a silver laptop.

"Who's this?" Mr. Hawaii said.

"Harry." My turtlenecked escort pointed at me. "The new delivery guy."

I waved.

"Package is in the back with Dog Face." He went back to his laptop as if that was all the information I needed.

Turtleneck motioned to a wooden door at the far end of the room. I nodded at him and traversed the terracotta toward an arched entrance. I imagined some kind of circus freak dog-faced boy waiting for me on the other side.

The wooden door creaked open, and a scene right out of a bad cop show spread out before me. A long, fold-out table was covered in clear plastic bags full of white powder. A thick guy in a button-up shirt with rolled-up sleeves was busy stuffing the bags into brief cases.

I stood there speechless, not believing my eyes. If I would've seen this room in a cop show, I would've laughed at how over the top it was, then made some sarcastic comment about how it would never be so obvious in a real life situation.

"Who are you?" The thick guy scowled at me, his hand reaching for something behind his back.

"Harry. They sent me back here." The words leapt out of my mouth in fast motion. "Dog Face. Um, someone named Dog Face has my package." I could hear my voice tremble.

The thick guy chuckled. "Yeah." He motioned to the corner of the room where a young guy leaned against the wall, engrossed in his cell phone. "We got a filthy animal back here."

The young guy shook his head and slid the phone in his pocket. A fedora, white T-shirt and khakis gave him the look of a hipster, art director. He grabbed a brick-sized, brown paper package from the table and strolled over as if he might spin and break into a series of smooth dance moves at any moment.

"I'm Clarence. They're just jealous of this." He motioned to his face. "Chick magnet, right?"

It was hard to argue. He looked like a guy you'd see in a shaving commercial or on a billboard.

He lifted the package to me. "You running deliveries for Ms. Callow now?"

"Yep." I grabbed the package, secretly testing the weight to see if it might have a bag of cocaine inside. It seemed the perfect weight. A nervous tremor went through me, and I swallowed hard. I stuffed it in my messenger bag as if it was burning my hand.

Steve was right. He was actually right about all this. I was delivering cocaine. I couldn't believe it. It seemed so absurd.

"What's your ride?" Clarence raised a brow.

"Oh," I fumbled. "Ferrari Spider."

He grinned. "Nice."

"Yeah," I said. "It's not really mine. It's kind of the delivery car."

He gave me a light punch on the shoulder. "Don't worry man, you'll get yours soon enough. I started out with deliveries last year. The money gets good fast. That Audi S7 out there is mine."

"Cool." I had no idea what an S7 was, but it sounded expensive. At the moment, however, cars meant nothing. Somehow I'd landed in the middle of a million dollar drug den, and I wanted out. A hollow sensation swirled in my stomach. It was time to leave. Fast. "Well, I better get going."

"Sure, man. Take it easy." He shook my hand and pulled me in for one of those cool-guy-in-a-club kind of hand shakes that ends with two pats on the back. "And don't let these guys stick you with a nickname."

"I won't." I said the words as if I had any power over what guys with guns wanted to name me. I turned and headed back through the main room towards the front door. It took every ounce of self-control not to run. Mr. Hawaii nodded, not even bothering to look up from his laptop as I walked past.

Turtleneck opened the front door as I drew near. "Be careful out there."

"Thanks." I headed out of the house and into freedom. I felt elated as I stepped off the front porch and away from the drug den. My thrill was cut short as two police cars came barreling down the street.

CHAPTER 19

All my muscles seemed to lock up simultaneously as the police cars headed my way. They weren't merely patrolling the street, they were driving with a purpose. Was I just paranoid, or were they coming right toward the drug house?

My stress level swelled to maximum, and my body seemed to move of it's own accord. I turned and headed for the next house over. There was a thin alleyway between the homes which to me looked like a great escape route.

The wall of juniper trees out front made for a good cover. I only hoped I could make the alley before the cops realized where I'd come from. I headed through a gap between the trees, and soon I was in the alleyway, trying to keep my walk as natural as possible.

My sensory abilities focused completely on the sounds going on behind me. The police cars skidded to a stop, and I heard several pairs of hard-soled cop shoes scramble onto the street. I dared not look back and lock eyes with any of them.

I made my way further down the alley. My shoulders were

tense, and I expected at any moment a cop would order me to freeze.

Bougainvillea vines spread over metal fencing that ran between the houses. A few more steps and the vines would conceal me from searching cop eyes. At that moment it became my favorite plant in the whole world. Right as I passed it, raised voices sounded at the front door of the drug house. Cops were barking out orders for everyone to get their hands behind their heads and get on the ground.

My legs begged me to break into a sprint, but that would immediately mark me as guilty. I kept my cool and continued to walk at a normal pace. Making it this far gave me hope with every step that I could escape.

It was hard to believe I'd just been in that house. If the cops had arrived a few seconds earlier, I would've had my hands behind my back, lying on the terracotta next to Turtleneck and Mr. Hawaii.

There was a thin break in the bougainvillea plant ahead just wide enough to look through. I decided to risk a quick peek.

A broad window granted a view of the main room I'd just left. The police were already searching and handcuffing the people I just met. Clarence, aka Dog Face, the pretty boy drug runner, was last in the line of soon-to-be felons. I couldn't help but stare for a moment, thinking how easily that could have been me. Through some sixth sense Clarence turned and locked eyes with me. I ducked as if he'd just shot a bullet my way. Would he say anything? Would he try to pin something on me to get himself off the hook?

A door opened behind me. I spun to find a middle-aged guy in a blue sweat suit and slicked-back hair. He stood in the side doorway of the house I'd been sneaking by.

He flinched as if surprised to find me there. "Who are you?"

I realized I was still ducking and must've looked ridiculous. I stood quickly. "Hi. Sorry about that, I dropped a quarter." A quarter? That's the best excuse I could come up with? He looked up and down the alley. "Were you knocking out here? I had the radio on."

"Yes." I answered quickly. "I figured no one was home so I was about to leave."

"Oh. Well, how can I help you?"

Great. Why did I have to say I knocked? Now I had to think up a reason and delay my getaway. "Um, I'm selling magazines. Would you like to buy a subscription?" Perfect. He'd shoot me down, and I could get out of here.

"Really?" He leaned back and scratched at his cheek. "You know, I miss having a good magazine around. Everything's digital now. It's just not the same."

Terrific. I found the one guy who's nostalgic for print. "Yep. Magazines are great." I had to figure out a way to lose this guy's sale so I could bolt. "You know, I'm not supposed to say anything, but they're running a big discount next week. I could stop by later when it's cheaper."

He waved his hand. "I wouldn't do that to you. Two trips for one sale? I was in sales for twenty years. Takes a lot of guts to go door to door." He stretched out his hand. "I'm George."

I shook his hand. "Harry. It's really no problem. I can come back."

"Nonsense." He pulled his wallet out and fished for his card. "Do you have a sheet to fill out? It's probably done on your phone these days. Through an app, right?" He chuckled.

"Yeah. Totally." I pulled out my phone not knowing how to bluff my way much further. Out of the corner of my eye I saw someone enter the alley. I snuck a quick glance. A police officer was heading our way. A wave of panic surged through me. Everything inside of me cried out to run.

"You got *Popular Mechanics*?" George said. "That was my favorite."

My prison story was writing itself.

What are you in for?

A subscription to Popular Mechanics.

Ooo, tough break.

"Yep, we have that one. Good choice." I was hitting random apps on my phone pretending to order magazines. The man noticed the approaching cop. "Hm. The police are here."

Sometimes verbalizing the obvious helped people deal with strange situations.

"Morning." The cop looked at each of us, his eyes resting on me for an uncomfortably long moment. "We've had a disturbance next door." He rested his hands on his belt, one hand directly above the grip of his pistol. "We're looking for eye witnesses. Do either of you live here?"

"I do." George looked at me as if fresh doubts about my salesman persona had surfaced.

"I'm selling magazines." I decided to stick with the charade. Might as well go down with the ship. I glanced at the drug mansion behind me as if just becoming aware of it. "What happened next door? Are we in danger?"

The cop searched my eyes a moment. "It's under control. How long have you been here selling magazines?"

I shrugged. "Not long. George here was ordering *Popular Mechanics*."

The cop looked at him. "Is that right?"

"Yes. What exactly is going on?" George looked at the drug house with narrowed eyes. "I've wondered about them. A lot of late night noises."

"Nothing to worry about. We've taken care of the situation." The cop looked at me for what seemed like an eternity. His eyes slid down to my messenger bag. "What's in the bag?"

My skin flared like it had caught fire. He had me. This was it. I was going to jail. The cocaine package was in my bag, waiting to reveal itself and cement my guilt. A numb feeling swept over me. I was about to admit everything but swear my innocence in the whole situation when a sudden thought hit me.

"Samples." I blurted out.

The cop's brow knitted like I was speaking another language.

"Magazine samples." I reached into my bag and pulled out my copy of *Car and Driver* magazine.

"Ah." The cop's posture switched from alert mode to boredom in nanoseconds. He glanced from George to me as if we were suddenly holding him up. "You got a copy of *Guns and Ammo*?"

"Um, yeah," I said. "I mean, not with me, but I can order it for you." I wanted to offer him a lifetime subscription if he'd just let me go.

The cop nodded. "You got a card or something?"

"Not yet. I can email you the subscription info if you'd like." I had no idea what I was doing anymore. I was treading water in a whirlpool.

His radio static sounded. A voice spit out a garbled string of numbers and clipped words. He picked up the radio. "Ten-four." He nodded at us. "You two have a nice day."

The cop turned and headed back down the alley. My heart was breakdancing with excitement.

"Weird." George was looking from the cop to the house next door.

"I know." I tried to match his fresh batch of concern. "What's going on with your neighbors?"

He shook his head. "I always knew something strange was happening over there."

An idea hit me like a lightning bolt. It had the potential to

be an expensive idea, but it was worth it. "Okay, I'll get you going on that subscription. Let me just—"
I faked a fumble with my phone and dropped it. It clattered to the ground. "Oh no!" I pretended to be really concerned and retrieved the phone, hitting buttons in a feigned panic.
"Did it crack?" George sounded sympathetic.
I looked forlorn at the screen and gave a dramatic sigh. "It's not responding. I think I broke it."
"Wow. Sorry about that," he said.
"Well, I was due for an upgrade." My three-year-old phone actually *was* due for an upgrade, so it was nice to mix some truth into this whole farce. I stuffed the phone in my pocket.
"Well, I'll have to come back for that subscription."
"Of course. Sorry about your phone."
"It's okay. Well, take care." With a quick wave I turned and headed down the alley toward freedom.
I trudged my way back through the winding roads of Naples to Second Street. There was no way I could go back to the Ferrari right now. If cops were gonna be swarming around the drug mansion confiscating drugs and dusting for prints, I didn't want to be anywhere near it. Especially since I'd already met one of the officers who would measure my magazine-salesman story against owning a Ferrari, and straight to prison I'd go.
Fifteen minutes of sidewalk brought me to the storefronts of Second Street. I spied a corner coffee shop that looked more like an antique store. After traversing untold blocks of the winding maze called Naples, it seemed like an oasis.
The front door had one of those ageless jingling bells that announced new customers. A heady aroma of fresh brewed coffee hit me like an enchanted breeze. I glanced down at my messenger bag. How tempting it was to throw the unmarked package, most likely filled with cocaine, in the trash. But wasn't

that how every panicked drug runner ended up dead? I had to hold onto it. I'd take it to Solas and that would be the end of things.

I bought and chugged a ridiculously expensive bottle of water to recover from the long walk. After several deep breaths at the front counter, the barista eyed me with concern and asked if I was feeling all right. I nodded and ordered a hot chocolate with extra whipped cream. Sure, it was a kids' drink, but after what I'd just been through, I could use a few moments of being a kid again.

A plush set of Wingback arm chairs by the window called my name. The chairs huddled around a wooden table with a chess board painted on top. I claimed one of the comfy seats as my own and relaxed into the velvet-covered cushions. I slid the messenger bag between my thigh and the chair, taking a quick glance around to make sure no one was watching me. It was like carrying around a bomb that could go off at any second.

My mind and body were exhausted. During the long walk through Naples, I'd obsessed over the repercussions of my near-prison experience. I'd gone from a simple delivery job to working with drug dealers, and I couldn't remember a time I'd spat out so many lies to get out of a jam.

One thing was clear, it was time to part ways with Solas. Hot as she was, and as connected to the comic book industry as she might be, every pickup and delivery she'd sent me on turned into a nightmare. No job was worth incarceration or death.

I let out a long exhale and leaned my head back against the chair. My life had spun pretty far out of control. How had it all happened so fast? It was time for a divine plea. I closed my eyes and sent up a prayer. It was a mix of apologies and a heartfelt request for help.

"About time." A familiar voice sounded beside me.

CHAPTER 20

I opened my eyes to find Finch sitting in the chair opposite me. He wore black jeans, an Izod Lacoste T-shirt and a Members Only jacket.

The chessboard was set up on the table in front of us.

He moved a pawn two spaces forward. "Your move."

"Finch! Thank God. I need help."

Finch huffed out a laugh. "Tell me about it." He grabbed a mug that looked identical to mine, right down to the whipped cream swirl. He took a sip and grimaced. "Ugh. So sweet. What are you? A six-year-old boy?"

I glared at him. "You know, for about two seconds I was happy to see you. It's amazing how fast you can annoy me." I moved a pawn forward on the chess board.

Finch grinned. "You deserve it for working with a demon."

I looked around to see if anyone was in earshot. Thankfully there were only a few scattered customers a healthy distance away. "Look, I don't know what she is, but I'm out. I'm giving her this final package and walking away."

He shook his head and slid his queen halfway up the board. "Bad idea. She's trouble. Best to never see her again."

"I have to give this back." I lifted the package out just enough so he could see it, then stashed it back in the bag. "It's like an anchor around my neck."

He nodded. "Yep, sin is like that."

"Hey, I'm innocent. She didn't tell me what I was picking up."

"Did you ask?"

I paused. He grinned.

"By the way." He pointed at the mug. "Just because it's a drink, this doesn't qualify as fasting."

"I never agreed to fasting."

He put up his hands. "Fine. Ignore my wisdom."

"Whatever." I brought my knight out. My skills at chess weren't bad. My uncle taught me at an early age, and I'd caught on quickly. Normally I'd be pretty confident with a new game, but if Finch actually was an angel, he could have centuries of game experience that would be difficult to match.

"I have a new mission for you." Finch moved his bishop.

"My plate's a little full right now." I slid a pawn forward.

"Won't take but a second." He moved his queen. "Check."

"What?" I studied the board. Unbelievable. He already had me on defense.

"You see that guy over there?" Finch pointed his queen at a sixty-ish guy in a grey suit by the corner window.

"Yeah." My focus snapped back to the chess board. Even though no one would ever believe me, beating an angel at chess would be a huge personal victory. As a block and to lure him into losing his queen, I brought out my second knight for reinforcements.

"Go talk to him." Finch moved his bishop again. "That's your mission."

I looked back at the older man. He gazed out the window

with a dream-like stare. An espresso cup and saucer sat motionless in his lap as if he'd forgotten about his drink.

"Why?" I said. "Who is he?"

Finch moved his queen again. "I can't tell you."

"Well, that's real mature." His queen and bishop were hedging me in. I slid out another pawn for added defense.

"Sometimes it's not about the *why*'s," he said. "Remember the old hymn, 'Trust and Obey'?"

"Hymns are boring." I took another sip of my hot chocolate. No matter what he said, it was delicious and comforting.

Finch shook his head. "You know, not so long ago young people had things called reverence and respect."

"Let me guess, during the eighties, right?"

He advanced his bishop. "Checkmate."

I leaned forward to study the board. No matter which way I tried to shuffle the pieces, there was no denying it. He had me.

"No fair." I looked up to charge him with cheating by distracting me with the old man, but Finch was gone. He was nowhere in sight. It was getting harder to deny his angelic abilities.

"Wait. Finch?" A thorough scan of the coffee shop came up empty. Even his hot chocolate was gone. If I'd known he was gonna vanish as fast as he appeared, I would've asked more questions.

I leaned back in my comfy chair and took a long drink of my chocolate. I took a wary side glance at the old man in the corner, who hadn't moved. I'd secretly hoped he might have left when I wasn't looking. What kind of mission was it to talk to some old guy in a coffee shop?

The text tone sounded on my phone. Solas.

> I heard what happened. I had no idea what my client was involved in. Completely unacceptable. Meet me at 12:30 for lunch at Magaris. I'll make it up to you.

Yeah, sure she didn't know. It was time to get out. Steak lunch or not, I wasn't going. Twelve thirty was already booked in my mental calendar for volunteering at Caring Tables. Those couple hours gave me a chance to stay connected with Amber. I still felt as if her getting hurt in the car accident was my fault. I couldn't wait to see her again and pick up where we left off.

I tapped out a return text.

> Thanks but it's not working out. I'm coming by your place soon. If you're not there, I'll leave the package with the concierge.

I turned my phone off and stuck it in my pocket. My mind was set, and I didn't want to hear any more of her explanations. After another long drink of chocolate, I set the cup down on the disappointing aftermath of the chess board and headed for the exit.

Halfway to the door, I paused. The old man in the corner, who I could see out of my peripheral vision, haunted me. Finch's "mission" nagged at my brain. What was I supposed to say to some random stranger? Finch didn't even give me a conversation starter.

I turned to study the old man a moment, pretending to browse a wooden shelf filled with classic novels. Peeking over a weathered copy of *Robinson Crusoe*, I tried to get an idea of who my "mission" was. Perfect posture, custom fitted grey suit, and well trimmed white hair and goatee. My guess was either ex-military or regimented executive. Most likely someone who'd led a disciplined, successful life. In other words, my complete opposite. The Bizzaro world version of me. What would I say to someone so different?

A rush of embarrassment went through me at the thought of talking to the guy. I had a strong urge to leave. To laugh off Finch's "mission" and just get on with my life. After all, I had places to go, things to do.

I took a step toward the exit and stopped. What was I really running from? It wasn't that difficult of a task. If Finch really was an angel giving me a divine mission, talking to a stranger wasn't a dangerous quest. After all, I talked to crazy Beck at the soup kitchen, this couldn't be any weirder.

I let out a deep breath and took purposeful strides toward the old man. My mind reeled with what I would say once I reached him. My conversation starters with strangers generally began with a full helping of awkward and got worse as they went.

It took only a precious few seconds until I was up in his space. He looked up as if brought out of deep thought.

"Hello." His eyes bounced from the front counter back to me. "Do you work here?"

"Um, no. I just, um, wondered if you wanted to talk." I tried a friendly smile, but I could feel it twitch it's way across my nervous face. No doubt I came off super creepy.

"Oh." His eyes narrowed a bit as if I was an old relative asking for money. "No. I'm fine. Thanks."

I held up my hands. "I don't blame you. This probably seems weird. I'm not a psycho or anything. See, my friend"—I pointed to the empty Wingback chairs and chessboard—"well, he's not here anymore, but we were playing chess and he beat me and then he said I should come talk to you." My voice was taking on a nervous ramble. Pretty soon the guy was probably gonna call for security. "I'm not sure why. I'm sorry to bother you."

"Oh. Lost a bet, did you?" He grinned as if he'd just solved my riddle.

I shrugged. "Something like that."

He motioned to the seat opposite him. "I have to leave in a few minutes, but you're welcome to sit. At least you can make good on your bet."

"Thanks." I sat down. "I'm Chris by the way."

"Phillip." He set his cup and saucer on the round table between us. He studied me for a minute. "Do you mind if I ask your age?"

"Twenty-one."

Phillip nodded. "My nephew is nineteen." He gazed out the window again. "I'm having trouble understanding your generation."

Oh boy. He was asking about "my generation." It always seemed strange to me that someone would ask my opinion about millions of strangers as if I was their spokesman. I didn't even understand half of my friends.

I decided to go with the hippie angle. It was vague and allowed me to avoid a thoughtful response. "Well, it's a tricky age. Most of us are just trying to figure out who we are."

"Mm." Phillip pursed his lips as if annoyed by my answer.

The poor guy let me interrupt his relaxing coffee moment, the least I could do was offer to bridge the generation gap. "Still, maybe I can help. What's the story with your nephew?"

Phillip turned from the window and met my eyes like he was giving me one last shot to hold his attention. "He's a concert pianist."

"Cool." It always amazed me how much other kids were able to accomplish during their childhood while I was playing video games.

"I took him to the Philharmonic several times." Phillip

ran his finger along the rim of the coffee cup, a subtle grin ran across his face, then quickly disappeared. "It seemed a mutual dream of ours that one day he would join them."

Overachiever. "Sounds great."

"Yes. I thought so. He's recently decided to devote his talent to rock and roll..." He studied me as if trying to gauge my reaction. "Seems an odd choice, don't you think?"

What was I gonna say? Honestly, it sounded kind of cool. There were some talented rockers out there that started out with classical training. But with disappointed Uncle Philharmonic over here, I was obviously going to land on the wrong side of this issue.

"Well, everybody's gotta find their path, right?" I tried.

"Mm." He stared out the window as if he wanted to lose himself in another daydream.

Why would Finch send me to this guy? I was making the situation worse.

"At least he's still using his musical talents," I said. "I mean, my mom wanted me to be a dentist, and I draw comics. Now that's disappointment."

Phillip frowned at me. "Comics?"

I pointed at him. "Yep, that's the look she gave me when I told her."

He smiled. "Sorry. It's just ... It's difficult when I see so much potential."

"I totally get it," I said. "It's like when they made those Star Wars prequels. Y'know, you're all excited because of the original trilogy and then you watch *Phantom Menace* and you just can't understand how it all went so wrong."

His face was void of expression as though I was speaking gibberish.

"Never mind," I said. "Maybe he would've been great in the Philharmonic but bored out of his mind. I'm sure you wouldn't want that for your nephew. Maybe rock is his true calling."

Phillip gave a lopsided grin. "And you think we all have some sort of true calling?"

"Maybe. Maybe it's not just one thing. I mean, I've been working at Caring Tables. You know, that soup kitchen up on Cherry Street?"

"Yes, I'm familiar with it."

"Right. Well, I'd never done that before, but it's been pretty amazing. I actually helped some people, and it got me out of my head for awhile. I'm going back all this week. Maybe there's callings like that every day. Things that put you in a different place than you thought. But better, you know? Maybe your nephew will end up in the Philharmonic, maybe not, but if he doesn't explore a little bit, he'll never know where he fits."

Phillip leaned back, his wooden chair creaking with the shifting weight. "Interesting."

I had to admit, I was kind of impressed with my own insights. It was rare my thoughts flowed with such rhythm.

He checked his watch. It was one of those sleek, silver watches like you see on luxury car commercials.

"Well, I must be going." He took another drink from his cup and stood, extending his hand. "Nice meeting you, Chris. I'm glad you stopped by to chat."

"Yeah, me too." I shook his hand like we'd just done a business deal. "Good luck with your nephew. Try to go easy on him."

"Indeed I will." He grinned and strode out of the store, the bell above the door signaling his departure.

I looked over at the coffee shop display case. Rows of pastries and breakfast-style sandwiches called out to me. My stomach grumbled in protest. I'd barely eaten all day. Aside from gluten free scones which I'm pretty sure didn't even count as food, the half cup of hot chocolate was my only nourishment of the day. I wasn't too keen on following

Finch's fasting advice. I'd never tried it, but it sounded like self-inflicted torture. Still, I was in a bad spot. Maybe it was worth a try.

My stomach rumbled again as if arguing with my thoughts. I decided to give fasting a go. At least for the rest of the day. Either I'd pass out or reach some kind of spiritual break through. With all the supernatural insanity flooding into my life, I needed to use every tool at my disposal. I resigned myself to the idea, feeling like an apprentice mountaintop monk.

It was time to face the music and end things with Solas. I called Steve, hoping to beg for another ride.

"Chris!" Steve sounded uncharacteristically peppy. "You're not gonna believe this."

"What's up?" I didn't know whether to feel excited or frightened.

"I just landed an amazing art gig."

"Sweet. How?"

"So, I was talking to our new neighbor Eddie this morning and—"

"Wait, homeless Eddie?" I interrupted.

"No, dude. I just told you he's our new neighbor, how can he be homeless?"

"Sorry. Formerly homeless."

"He moved from his sisters garage. What the heck you talking about?"

"I meant he was at Caring Tables and, oh, never mind," I said.

"Whatever. Anyway, I showed him my art, which he loved, and he said he knew a guy who did a kitchen remodel for some art dealer way up on Signal Hill. Apparently the art dealer was short on local artists for an exhibit tonight."

"I like where this is going."

"Exactly. So Eddie put in a call, I sent over pics of my paintings, and bam. I'm in the exhibit tonight."

"Dude, that's amazing!"

"I know, right?" Steve was practically hyperventilating. "I'm getting my stuff together to set up. Lots of wealthy art lovers show up at this thing from what I hear. If all goes well, rent might not be an issue for a while."

"Awesome, man. You deserve it." I was genuinely happy for Steve. As much as I teased him about his work, I always admired his talent and dedication to it. Plus, I knew how hard it was for an artist to get their stuff out there.

"You've gotta come tonight," Steve said. "I'll call you later with details."

The connection clicked off. Obviously his brain was moving a million miles an hour. With his usual mellow demeanor, I almost didn't know how to talk to him when he was that amped up. Either way, asking for a ride was out of the question. Time for another Uber request.

My one and only credit card was getting a good workout today, with coffee shop drinks and Uber rides. After paying my driver and giving serious thought to shuttling people around as a side job, I stared up at the gleaming structure of Silver Towers.

A stale breeze moved the late summer air around the way a government employee processes files. My fingers tightened around the messenger bag that held the dreaded brown package within. Having made it this far, nothing was going to stop me from completing my delivery, leaving this job, and living the drug free life once more.

I entered the lobby through the stately, smudge free glass doors, and headed for the front desk. The snooty concierge was gone. I reached the front counter and waited a few moments, but no one came. There were no telltale signs of employees chatting in the back room or crinkling snack bags during a break. It was quiet. The type of quiet I'd expect at three in the morning, not the middle of a sunny day.

"Hello?" I called out.

No answer. A light ding sounded, and the silver doors of the elevator slid open. The car was empty. I strolled over and peered inside. A key was inserted next to the button for penthouse access. Did Solas forget her key?

There was nothing stopping me from heading up and getting this whole thing over, in person. I hesitated. Quitting would be awkward, that was certain, but there was something else holding me back. Maybe Finch just got in my head, and I was imagining demons around every corner.

I craned my neck to check for the concierge. The front counter remained vacant.

"Oh, this is stupid," I said aloud to break out of my paranoia. A confident stride took me into the elevator, and I hit the button. The doors closed tight, and the elevator glided up to the penthouse.

CHAPTER 21

As the elevator hummed its upward ascent, I focused on the artwork gracing the silver doors. Seagulls were frozen in relief, as if they flew over palm trees by the ocean. I found myself jealous of their freedom and carefree existence.

A ding sounded, and the doors slid open. The serene, cloud-like decor of Solas's penthouse spread out before me. The faint smell of vanilla welcomed me in. Soft music floated down from the overhead speakers. The harmonious strains were full of chimes and stringed instruments, and I felt as if I'd just stepped into a spa.

"Chris? Is that you?" Solas sat in the lotus position by the floor-to-ceiling windows. Sunlight poured in on her and two brunette women sitting close by. They all wore flowing white gowns and formed a loose triangle. Several sticks of incense burned beside them, the sluggish curls of smoke drifting upward.

"Hey." I gave an awkward wave. "I brought your package."

"Come on over." Solas stood, the sun revealing the silhouette of her gym-perfect body through the sheer material. She moved toward me with the smooth confidence of someone who rarely tastes rejection.

I took a few hesitant steps forward, stopping by the oversized quartz counter island that separated the kitchen from the sprawling living room.

Solas met me at the island. She gave a slow sigh, running a hand through her hair as if waking from a relaxing sleep. "I'm glad you're here."

Her beauty and casual confidence were disarming. It was hard to think straight. It was completely foreign to my life experience to be on close terms with a rich model.

I cleared my throat. "Nice, um, dress."

"Chemise." She smiled.

I'd never heard of a chemise before, but the soft, flowing material left little to the imagination.

A warning signal went off in my head. I needed to snap out of it. But there was a desperate battle of logic versus lust going on in my mind, and it seemed logic was drowning.

"Hope I didn't interrupt." I pointed to the two brunettes still sitting by the window. "You guys doing a seance or something?"

"We're gathering for spiritual connection," Solas said.

"Oh. What religion are you?"

"We avoid organized religion. We use truths from all faiths to help us connect spiritually."

I nodded, not really sure what that meant. "So, what do you do when the different faiths don't agree with each other? Flip a coin?"

She shook her head as if dismissing the thought. "We don't focus on conflict. We only use positive forces to achieve spiritual oneness. The true nature of the divine can be found within."

It was all sounding pretty hippie-dippie, so I decided to move on. "Here." I grabbed the package from my messenger back and handed it to her. At the very least, I wanted that off my hands.

"Thank you." She took it with one hand and placed the other hand on my shoulder, moving in close. "I apologize for what you went through. I honestly had no idea what my client was involved in."

Her clear, blue eyes pleaded innocence, but at this point my logic was screaming at me.

"Look, it's none of my business." I took a step back to gain some distance. "Maybe your clients aren't leveling with you. The cops were all over that place. I almost got arrested. I had to leave the Ferrari there." I handed her the car keys. "Here. I don't want to go back. I don't want to deliver drugs anymore."

It felt good to say it out loud. Almost like I was freeing myself from the association.

"Drugs?" She chuckled. "Is that what you think this is?" She waved the package in the air.

"Well ..., yeah."

She shook her head like I was a naive child and unwrapped the package. Inside was a wooden box. "Whatever my clients were into on the side has nothing to do with my deliveries." She opened the box and pulled out a smoked glass figurine of a butterfly.

"A butterfly?" Suddenly I felt very stupid.

Solas nodded. "This is an Alcon blue. Isn't it beautiful?"

I nodded, not knowing what to say.

She held the figurine up to the light, turning it over in admiration. "I lived in Europe for a few years. There was a field near my home full of them."

"It just seemed ..." I struggled for the words. "I thought..."

She moved close, putting a finger on my lips. "It's okay. I

understand. The important thing is that we learn from this and move forward. I really like you. I think we'll be great together."

She leaned in and pressed her soft lips against mine. I hesitated for a moment, lost in the shock and pleasure of the kiss. The face of Amber rushed into my thoughts, and I stepped away. "Um, I can't. Listen, I need to leave."

Her brows turned downward as if I'd hurt her. "What's wrong?"

"I'm sort of seeing someone," I blurted out.

"Oh." She seemed unphased. "You never mentioned it. Is it serious?"

"Well, we haven't actually been on a date. Not officially anyway."

She smirked. "Then what's the problem? If you're not exclusive, then you haven't broken any commitments."

She was making a lot of sense and easing my conscience, but I couldn't get over a nagging feeling of betrayal. "Maybe. Either way, I need to stop doing deliveries for a while."

Her face tightened. "Hold on a sec." She turned to the other women. "Let's take a break, ladies."

The two brunettes stood and turned our way. They were stunning. Since their backs were to us before, I hadn't realized how gorgeous they were.

They made their way over like models on a catwalk, which was probably what they did for a living. The brunettes shot me seductive looks and slinked into the next room.

"You should join us." Solas weaved around me, heading into the kitchen. "We're going in the jacuzzi." She grabbed a clear bottle of vodka from the freezer and a couple shot glasses. "Things could get a little wild, but I'm sure you won't mind."

"Um, I don't know," I managed.

She put the glasses on the counter. "Look, a lot has happened today. I understand if you want to take a break from deliveries." She filled the shot glasses with the clear liquid.

"Why don't you take the rest of the day to think about it. No need to rush your decision." She lifted her glass. "First, have a drink with me."

I paused for a moment, staring at the shot glass in front of me. My thoughts were muddled. Part of me wanted out. Completely out. To cut ties with Solas and never look back. That was my intention up until I set foot in this penthouse. The other part of me, the part that was gaining ground fast, was begging me to stay. My inhibitions were dropping by the second, and I knew that shot of vodka would probably make my decision for me.

"I'm not much of a vodka guy." It was actually the truth. Had she poured tequila, things might have been more precarious.

She chuckled. "It's just one drink, Chris." She threw back the shot and winked. "Think about it. I'll be right back."

Solas headed into the next room where the brunettes went. Desire surged within me to follow her. My mind tried desperately to churn out justifications for staying. There seemed so many good excuses I could use to explain myself later.

A strange thought hit me. Why now? Why at this moment was an over-the-top temptation dangled in front of me. Had I really been seeing angels and demons the last couple days? If so, wouldn't this be somehow connected?

I imagined myself walking into the next room. Did I really want to be that guy? Deep down I knew I'd be selling out. Selling out my convictions and the faith I claimed to follow. Plus, I couldn't imagine looking Amber in the eye afterwards. I threw up a desperate prayer. *God help me.*

My phone rang. It was Amber.

"Hey." I was filled with guilt even though I hadn't done anything ... yet.

"Hey, Chris," Amber said. "I'm at Caring Tables. Got here a little early to help with the lunch rush. You still coming?"

The time on my phone read 12:03. "Um, yeah. Pretty sure."

"Great," she said. "Looks like we've got a full house today. Just want to make sure we have enough staff."

A voice in the background called her.

"Gotta go," she said. "See you soon."

She sounded so happy and wholesome. I, on the other hand, felt like a huge perv.

My phone clicked off. I gazed at the kitchen trash can nearby thinking I belonged in there. Something familiar caught my eye. I moved closer and dug through crumpled up napkins and a banana peel to discover my art pad. I gasped as I drew it out, brushing off wet coffee grounds. I flipped through the first pages only to confirm the awful truth. It was my graphic novel. All my original artwork.

Solas strolled back into the kitchen. "So, you ready to join us."

The lustful hold she had on me only a moment ago was gone. I held up my art pad, my eyes narrowing at her. "What is this?"

She hesitated only for a second, a trace of worry in her eyes, before assuming her usual smooth demeanor. "Don't worry, I made copies. I told you it needed proper formatting."

"These are my original sketches. You don't just throw it away!" The concentrated effort of all those late nights working hard to make every panel tell a dynamic action story welled up within me. It was like someone threw my dreams in the trash.

She shrugged. "There were errors that couldn't go to print. Smudges, imperfections. I'm having them fixed at my printing service. You should be thanking me."

"Really? Where are they? I want to see them." I wasn't letting it go this time. Something had changed. Somehow I knew she was lying.

She titled her head with a condescending look. "Now, Chris.

This is silly. We'll talk about this later. Come on, the girls are waiting in the other room."

"Where's the keys to my motorcycle?" I said.

"Chris, just relax."

I scanned the kitchen. There was a row of silver pegs by the fridge with key rings. My motorcycle keys hung on one of them. "I'm leaving. No more deliveries." I strode to the fridge and snatched my keys off the peg.

"Chris." Her look and tone turned serious. "If you leave, it's over. I don't give second chances."

"Fine." My original conviction rushed back. If I stuck with her, I'd end up in jail or dead, and those deep blue eyes of hers would just blink with feigned innocence and pin the blame on me. I wanted freedom.

I marched past her, heading for the elevator. "Goodbye Solas."

"Oh, Chris?" She called after me.

"Yeah." I didn't break stride.

"I'd stay away from that soup kitchen if I were you."

I stopped. An empty sensation grew in my gut. Something in her tone had changed. I craned my neck back. "What'd you say?"

She watched me like a cat eyeing a canary. "It's not your fight. Just stay out of the way, and you won't get hurt."

I turned back to face her, my chest tightening as a wave of anxiety washed over me. "What's any of this got to do with the soup kitchen? I never even mentioned it."

"Just don't get involved." The warm and flirtatious tones ever present in her voice were gone. In their place was a cold certainty. The voice of someone in authority with power to enforce their will. "You have no concept of the forces at work here."

I searched her eyes, having trouble connecting her speech with the person who was so different a moment ago. "Are you threatening me?"

"Yes." The pupils of her eyes grew until there was nothing behind her lids but a glossy blackness. I froze, my muscles tensing.

Solas blew me a kiss. A thick stream of black smoke poured out of her mouth and ran across her fingers. The smoke dropped to the floor as if it had weight. It spread across the white marble, painting the floor with dark tendrils that slithered forward.

I took a few reflexive steps back, my heart pounding. My outrage disappeared. All that was left was a primal fear of the unknown.

The pleasant warmth of the room was gone. Goosebumps covered my skin as the air turned chill. I hugged my arms, suddenly feeling like I'd stepped into the arctic.

A bell sounded behind me. The silver elevator doors opened. I rushed through into the carriage and pressed the garage button over and over, praying the doors would close and take me away from this place.

Solas stood watching me. Dark tendrils swirled around her like ethereal serpents. The black mist covered the walls and floor of the entire penthouse with creeping tendrils drawing close. I pressed my body flat against the back of the elevator, taking in a sharp breath. The doors slid closed just before the darkness poured in.

I slumped to the floor of the elevator as it descended. My body was trembling. At any moment I expected the smoky tendrils to flow through the cracks of the elevator and consume me. Nothing I'd experienced in life had prepared me for the terror I felt at that moment.

The elevator bell sounded and the doors opened. I sprinted into the garage, searching desperately for my bike. My eye caught the glint of fluorescent lighting on the familiar black gas tank nearby. I hopped on my motorcycle and kick-started the engine to life.

I glanced back toward the elevator. There was no black smoke or anyone coming after me, but I couldn't shake the sense of being followed. I cranked the throttle and rocketed out of the parking garage as if the whole place might explode at any moment.

CHAPTER 22

◆

It wasn't until the wind battered against me at fifty miles an hour that my numbness wore off. I wove my motorcycle through traffic on Seventh Street as if someone or something was chasing me. For all I knew, something was.

Finding my motorcycle in the underground parking structure of the Silver Towers and flooring it out of there was like escaping prison. I couldn't get the last vision of Solas out of my head. The swirling black mist coiling around her limbs and those glassy black eyes staring into my soul was an experience that promised to haunt my nightmares. It wasn't just the sight of her transformation, there was something else. Something beyond the physical realm that awakened a sense of horror I'd never known. A deep fear like a child exposed to a gruesome murder. I couldn't remember the last time I'd felt so alone and defenseless.

Any doubt that I'd set foot into the supernatural world was gone. I was in a new, terrifying reality where my mortal life seemed insignificant to the spiritual powers surrounding me.

I had to see Amber. She was my antidote to Solas. The light after the flood of darkness. Of course, that meant I was headed straight for Caring Tables. The very place Solas warned me to stay away from. A smarter man would pay attention to a black-eyed minion of the devil. But I couldn't. I knew it deep down. Any other choice at this moment would be selling out in a way I knew I'd never fully recover from.

I turned on Cherry Street and cranked the throttle, powering out of the turn. All I needed to do was reach Caring Tables and see Amber's face. Then the hurricane of anxiety spinning through my gut would go away. Or at least diminish.

A pillar of black smoke rose in the distance. My first thought was a smoke-stack belch from an old factory. Only there were no factories in this part of the city. As the street signs blurred by, I realized a terrible truth. The dark smoke was rising from Caring Tables.

A fire engine blocked the front entrance of the soup kitchen. I pulled up behind the bright red behemoth, a hollow sensation in my stomach. The pane glass window of the store front was shattered. A spray of glass fragments and ash littered the sidewalk. Fire fighters in yellow turnouts carried charred tables and chairs from the building like wounded soldiers from a battlefield.

Grey smoke slithered from the blackened hull of the building. There was no sign of lingering flames. The warm, stifling air made it hard to breath. I pulled my shirt up over my mouth to keep from coughing.

I spotted Amber sitting on the curb half a block past the fire engine. I parked my bike and hurried over. She was crying with her head on Heath's shoulder. Heath had his arm around her, his gaze fixed on the horizon.

"Amber? You okay?" I said.

She looked up, her eyes red from tears. She jumped up and embraced me, a fresh batch of tears moistening the side of my neck.

Heath nodded at me, his expression blank as if he'd just finished a twelve hour shift. "They hit us with Molotov cocktails."

"Who?" I said.

He shrugged. "Who knows? City thugs. Not everyone likes what we're doing here."

I scanned the street. "Where's the police?"

"Out back." Amber lifted her head, speaking through tears. "We're supposed to stay till they finish looking around. We couldn't tell them much. We didn't see who did this."

"No one saw anything?" I said.

"One of the homeless guys saw a car but no plates," Heath said. "A grey El Camino. Not a lot for the cops to go on."

"What?" A creeping sensation coursed through me. I locked eyes with Amber. "That's the same kind of car that hit us."

Amber had a blank look. "An El Camino?"

"A *grey* El Camino." My heart sped up with the connection of events. "Just like the one that tried to run me down on the crosswalk, too. It's not a coincidence anymore."

Her eyebrows squinched together. "I don't understand. Is someone after you?"

"Apparently."

"Who?" she said. "And why would they go after the soup kitchen?"

I threw up my hands. "I don't know. My life stopped making sense a few days ago."

Heath stood, studying me like a concerned shrink. "Someone is after you? Is everything all right?"

Amber fixed me with serious eyes. "Yeah, what's going on, Chris?"

"Nothing. I'm not into anything weird or illegal ... At least, not anymore."

Heath shared an uneasy look with Amber.

"Whatever it is, you can tell us, man," Heath said. "Addictions cause paranoia. I've seen it. Just let it out, bro. We can help."

"No, no." I put up my hands, deflecting the charge. "I'm not into drugs. I mean, this morning I was at a drug house, but I didn't know it was a drug house, so I got out of there fast and—"

"A drug house?" Amber's mouth went slack.

Heath put his hand on my shoulder. "Chris, we can get you the help you need."

I shook my head. "I promise, I don't need help."

He gave a sympathetic nod. "That's what everyone says."

"No, listen, it's not like that." I swatted his hand from my shoulder. "I've never done drugs. Well, except this one time with a joint, but it was just a quick puff."

Amber frowned at me.

"Here's the thing," I said. "I was running deliveries for this woman. Well, turns out she's not a woman she's actually ... never mind, long story, anyways—"

"Chris." Amber drew closer to Heath. "You're starting to freak me out."

"I'm fine," I said. "Honest."

"Listen." Amber's voice took on a slow, concerned cadence like she was talking me off a ledge. "My church has a great recovery program. Counseling, support groups, you name it. They could really help."

"Yeah." Heath pulled a card from his pocket. "Chris, you should take this."

It was a business card for a doctor.

"Dr. Plinse is unreal," Heath said. "He runs the program. Addiction, counseling, recovery. He helped me break pain meds after a surf injury."

"Definitely," Amber said. "You should really go see him."

It was all I could do not to explode. With the insane events of the day piling up, I was at my wits end. I'd come here for relief only to find my new sanctuary burned and my new almost girlfriend so afraid of me that she was headed back to the comforting arms of ex-boyfriend Heath. I had to fix this.

"Listen to me. I'm clean," I spoke in the calmest voice I could muster. "I was running deliveries I thought were legit, but there were shady people working there. Maybe they're after me, I don't know, but I'm innocent."

Heath gave a patronizing grin. "We're here for you, bro. Just give Dr. Plinse a call ... Sometimes the demons are after us 'cause we fed them in the first place."

He was like a bad Yoda for druggies. It was hard to tell if he was actually trying to help or wanting me to look the fool in front of Amber. At that moment I really wanted to knock that smug surfer grin off his face.

An officer with a grey crew cut walked up to us. "We need to ask a few more questions." His eyes bounced between the two of them.

"We'll talk later." Amber put Dr. Plinse's business card in my hand. "Please give the doctor a call."

"I don't need a doctor," I said.

Amber grabbed my arm. "Just think about it." She turned and followed after the officer.

"Take care, Chris," Heath gave me a pat on the shoulder as he walked by.

The officer led them away, and I was left alone on the ash strewn sidewalk wondering how it all went so wrong.

CHAPTER 23

On the way back to my apartment it started to rain. And why not? Things were terrible, so the rain was only fitting. The worst thing about having a motorcycle as your only source of transportation was rainy days. Unless of course you live where it snows. Having grown up in the eternal summer of Long Beach, California, I had no reference for bikers in snowy climates, but my guess was they had it much worse.

By the time I pulled up to my apartment, I was drenched. Thankfully, I had a compartment under the bike seat where my cell phone and art pad stayed nice and dry. Grabbing my original sketches brought back a fresh wave of anger at finding them in the trash. Solas had lied to me from the beginning. Who knew how long she would have strung me along with promises of publication. Probably long enough until I wound up dead on one of her deliveries.

I still had trouble believing my last vision of Solas. How could it possibly be real? The incident seemed more like a horror scene from a movie. How could I accept anything I'd experienced over the last few days? If I told anyone about it, they'd think I was insane. At this point if someone told me I was a test subject in a hallucinogenic drug experiment, I'd be so relieved I wouldn't even get mad. I'd just thank them that it was all fake.

I ducked into my apartment to escape from the rain, only to face the suffocating heat within. The windows had been shut all day with the devil heater still going strong. The leaves of the lone living greenery in our apartment, a creeping charlie hanging over the sink, were curled and shriveled. A testament to the hostile living environment of our dwelling.

My soaked shoes were the first to go. I ditched them by the front door and made a beeline to my room for dry clothes. Normally the warmth would've been a nice counter to my water-logged condition. But the lack of fresh air, coupled with damp skin, turned my room into a muggy rain forest.

I threw open the windows and after a few minutes, the fresh rainstorm air made things livable once more.

After a change of clothes and a towel through my hair, I collapsed on my bed. I stared at the points and dips in the popcorn ceiling above me. It usually brought to mind the surface of the moon, but with what I'd been through, everything seemed alive. Shapes materialized in the texture. I could believe faces of dark creatures had always been there, only now I could see them clearly. I shut my eyes and prayed. I'd experienced enough fear today without my ceiling piling on.

My cell phone rang and my body jerked awake. The late afternoon light seeping through the blinds told me I'd fallen into some kind of stress-induced coma-like sleep for several hours.

I grabbed the phone from my plastic milk crate that pulled double duty as a bookcase and nightstand. A call from Solas.

My shoulders tensed. I stared at the phone as it rang. No way was I gonna answer that. I threw my cell into a pile of clothes on the other end of the room. What would it take to get rid of this woman, or demon, or whatever she was?

I heard the front door open and footsteps enter.

"Steve, is that you?" I said.

There was no answer. After a few moments, the footsteps approached my bedroom door. The doorknob turned and stopped. I'd locked the door before I got dressed. The knob rattled as someone tried to open it.

"Steve?" I called out.

A loud pounding on the door made my heart jump. I jolted out of bed, praying it was Steve.

"Who is it?" I tried to make my voice sound deeper ... and tougher.

No one answered. In two seconds I retrieved an aluminum bat from under my bed. A barely-used symbol of my one season in a softball league.

I tightened my grip on the bat, my whole body tensing in expectation.

There was a crash at the door like a rhino had charged it, followed by a splintering of wood. My door swung open, slamming against the opposite wall.

A big guy with arms covered in tattoos stood in the doorway brandishing a sledgehammer.

I instantly regretted throwing my phone across the room. If there was ever a time to call 9-1-1, this was it. The only reason I hadn't dropped the bat was that fear froze my hands on the grip. My mind was having trouble coping with the situation. The only thought that surfaced at that moment was recognition of the intruder. Trench. The same guy that clocked me at the ATM. The same guy that worked for Solas in the warehouse.

Trench locked eyes with me. There was an emptiness

there. Cold and determined. Translucent heat waves mixed with streams of black smoke flowed up from his shoulders as though his back was burning from some otherworldly fire.

His jaw clenched, and he marched toward me. I broke through my wall of fear and mustered enough courage to swing my bat at him. Without breaking stride Trench swatted it away with the sledgehammer and grabbed me by the throat with his free hand. He clamped down hard, and pain shot through my neck. It felt like my esophagus was collapsing. I choked and suddenly felt desperate for air.

I dropped the bat and grabbed at his fingers, trying to pry them free. He sent the head of the sledgehammer into my gut. Any oxygen left in my system disappeared. I cried out and doubled over. He released my neck and let me crumple to the floor.

My body heaved as I gasped for breath. Powerful hands gripped my shirt, wrapping it tight across my chest, and hoisted me back up. All my energy was directed toward regaining oxygen and coping with the pain. Fighting back wasn't anywhere on my list of options.

Trench flung me like a bag of sand through my bedroom doorway. I stumbled, and my shoulder caught on the doorframe, sending a burst of pain across my collarbone. My body spun, and after a few awkward steps, I face planted on the ten-year-old grey carpet in the living room.

A chill hit me like I'd just been thrown into a snow drift. The living room was freezing. A mocking, feminine laugh sounded nearby. I craned my sore neck to find the source. The room was abnormally dark, as if someone had hung black curtains over the windows. A thin layer of grey smoke, like a living thing, crept along the floor and walls. I blinked a few times, my eyes attempting to adjust.

Several candles sprang to life around the room as if lit simultaneously. The flames were a ghostly white instead of orange. Solas sat on Steve's art stool, glaring down at me. She was clad in a black gown with intricate lace designs like something out of a Bram Stoker novel.

"I thought I told you to stay away from that soup kitchen." Her deathly pale skin was a stark contrast to her blackened eyes.

Trench strode back into the room, taking his place at Solas' side. The sinews on his forearms flexed and released as he adjusted his grip on the sledgehammer. I felt like the railroad spike he was about to pound into the earth.

CHAPTER 24

My skin shivered in the cold. I sat up and hugged my arms for warmth. My breath came out in white puffs. It had to be about ten degrees in here.

Fear poured through me. I wanted to run. I glanced back at the front door of the apartment. A thick curtain of smoke swirled around it. Even if I made a break for it, I sensed I couldn't get through.

"What do you want?" My voice was shaking but I found the strength to speak. I forced myself to stare down her black eyes. "I don't work for you anymore."

Her lips went into a thin smile. "I'm going to make this simple, Chris." She said. "Leave this fight. Forget about the soup kitchen, and you can have your old life back. You'll never see me again."

"Or what?" I said. "You'll kill me?"

"I could've done that already." She flicked her eyes at Trench. "I have dozens of men like Trench here that wouldn't hesitate."

Trench gripped the sledgehammer firmly as if waiting for the word to attack me again.

"But I've been holding them back," she said. "Do you know why?"

I shook my head.

"Because I'm not your enemy," she said. "Tell me, the other angel you've been listening to, has he kept you safe?"

It was hard to deny that Finch had made things more complicated, even dangerous at times. "Not exactly."

"And since we've met," she said. "What did I do except offer the things you needed? A nice car to drive, a beautiful woman to admire"—she ran her hand down her body—"a job so you could pay bills." She flung a stack of money that landed by my knee. The smoke cleared upon impact, revealing a twenty dollar bill on the outside of the stack.

"That's two thousand," she said. "Just like I promised."

I stared at the large stack of cash, a thrill going through me at the idea of so much money at my fingertips.

"All this"—Solas motioned to the smoke and candles—"is a show. Just like at my penthouse. Sometimes these displays of strength are the only thing that will open your eyes to the truth."

"Oh?" I said. "What truth is that?"

"That I'm the one in control. My work is going to be accomplished one way or another. Those that stand aside will live, and those that don't will suffer their own bad choices."

I didn't know how to process such a crazy warning. I didn't know how to process anything I was experiencing. If it wasn't for the pain radiating from my recently sledgehammered stomach, my throbbing neck, and my doorway-clipped shoulder, I might have thought I was still dreaming.

"If you have so much power," I said, "why go to all this trouble? I mean, all this for a little hole-in-the-wall soup kitchen?"

"It's the first domino that has to fall," she said. "Once it goes, it will trigger other events. Events that will expand my power and influence. Events this city has been heading toward for years. You can try to stop it, but you're only delaying the inevitable. Whether it's good or bad depends on your perspective. Frankly, after thousands of years, I've lost interest in such distinctions. I'm here to complete a task. If I don't, others will finish it. But while I'm making final preparations, I can still warn people like you not to get swept away when the storm hits. I doubt the other angel you've been speaking to would give you the same chance."

A part of me, a large part, wanted to agree with everything she said. After all, this was beyond me. This was a level of supernatural for the angels to fight over. Even if I took a stand, what would that do, other than invite a worse beating?

"Do yourself a favor," Solas said. "Get out of this city for a while. Go back to your simple life. Find another girl to chase."

I'd been considering her perspective until that moment. "Wait, are you talking about Amber?"

"She's committed to a dying cause." Solas held up her hands in resignation. "We've tried to persuade her, but some people are too devoted for their own good."

A spark of anger lit a warmth in my chest. "So, what are you saying? Something bad will happen to her?"

"I wish no ill upon her." Solas put her hands to her heart. "But she's lost in her own ideals. It's not like she hasn't been warned."

I stood to my feet, a fire of outrage against her threats flowing through me. "Leave her alone. All she does is good for other people."

"Good, bad, everyone is a mix," she said. "Everybody is guilty of something."

A sudden impulse hit me. "Except Jesus."

Her eyes turned wild, and her face tightened, but a split second later, a mask of calm returned. "Careful, Chris. Don't walk into a fight you can't win."

She was right. I was in over my head. I prayed a desperate prayer. A plea for rescue from an impossible situation. I imagined myself begging at the feet of Jesus. Reaching out for his robe as if I were a leper on some ancient, dusty road.

At that moment, a strange sense of calm washed over me. For a second I thought stress had snapped something inside, and my body had gone numb. But I wasn't numb, I wasn't disconnected from the situation. I sensed everything around me just as before. Only now, a feeling of strength flowed through me. My memory flashed back to when Finch appeared in my car and warned me about demons.

"What?" I said. "You don't want me to call upon the power of Jesus?"

Her eyes narrowed, and a manic twitching animated her tight-lipped grimace as if she wanted to scream at me but was holding it in. A swarm of bright lights shone through the darkened windows as if flashlights were circling the apartment. Somehow I knew the light was power. A power I could access if I wanted. All I had to do was ask for it.

"Solas"—I spoke her name feeling a strength beyond me—"by the power of Jesus Christ, leave this place."

She shrank back in the chair, her fists clenched. "You little maggot. I'll tear you apart. I'll make Amber taste pain like never—" She looked toward the street as if suddenly distracted, then back at Trench. "Police. Get out of here."

Trench ran toward me, throwing his considerable body weight into me. He flung me sideways. I gratefully landed on the awaiting couch, and it broke my fall. He fled out the front door.

Solas glared at me. "You have no idea what you've started. You want to stand against the powers of hell? So be it!" The dark smoke from the apartment gathered around her and seemed to consume her body. It streamed out through the windows into the night air taking the bitter cold with it.

My body filled with warmth. Even though I'd just been body-checked into my couch, I felt triumphant. A relieved laughter spilled out of me. At that moment, I noticed the thick stack of bills still lying on the living room floor. I grabbed the stack, trying to remember if I'd ever held so much cash at one time.

I stuffed the bills in a brown lunch sack and put it in the back of the freezer. For some reason it seemed like the safest place.

A knock sounded at the front door, making my heart pound.

"Who is it?" I said.

"Long Beach Police," a muffled voice said. "We've had reports of a disturbance."

I checked through the peep hole and was relieved to see a police uniform.

Apparently, my brand new, previously homeless neighbor Eddie heard a loud crashing from my apartment and called the police, for which I would be eternally grateful.

After twenty minutes of questions, I gave a detailed description of Trench and Solas. Luckily the cop put forward the idea of robbery for the motivation of the break-in to which I offered no argument. This allowed me to conveniently leave out any discussion of sketchy deliveries around town. Of course, I also avoided details about dark smoke and demons. I needed the police on my side.

The cop took dutiful notes and examined the sledgehammered bedroom door before leaving. He seemed pretty bored with the whole thing. Apparently break-ins and sledgehammers were par for the course with law enforcement.

Moments after the cops left, my phone rang. A flood of relief hit me when the image of Steve covered the screen. A friendly face was sorely needed right now.

"Steve!" I said. "Man, do I need to talk to you."

"Hey," Steve said. "I'm at the exhibit, setting up. You still coming?"

"Oh, right." My brain was spinning. What was I going to tell him about the apartment? Would he even believe it? The only evidence was my damaged bedroom door. And the money in the freezer.

"You're coming, right?" Steve brought me out of my haze.

"Yeah, yeah. Of course."

"Cool. The view from this house is sublime. I can see the whole city from here. I had to borrow my dad's sport coat to class up my look a little. But that's it. It's still T-shirt and jeans underneath. I'm no sell out."

Steve was rambling which was definitely out of the norm. Obviously he was on cloud nine. Even in my current crisis, I couldn't help feeling happy for him.

"When does it start?" I said.

"Eight o' clock. I'll text you the address and the gate code," Steve said. "I have to finish my display, but I have a couple minutes. You said you wanted to talk about something?"

Of course I wanted to unload the full account of crazy I'd been through today, but how could I ruin his moment of triumph? I decided to give him the abbreviated version and wait till after the exhibit for a full download.

"Let's just say there's some wild spiritual stuff going on. I mean, extreme wild insanity level stuff," I said. "Plus Amber thinks I'm some kind of druggie now, so I could really use some prayer."

"For sure, man. For sure," he said. "By the way, I invited

Julie, and you'd think I'd asked her to go to Paris. Apparently she had a dress in her closet just itching for a nice event like this. Hey, you should invite Amber. She might get a better opinion of you in a tie and slacks instead of a superhero shirt."

He had a point. Maybe I could get on Amber's good side again with a classy night out. "That's not a bad idea."

"Yeah," Steve said. "Plus, on the drive over, she'll be a captive audience. That'll give you a chance to straighten things out."

"It's worth a shot."

"Cool. See you tonight."

I clicked off the phone and retrieved the business card Heath gave me for the head doctor. As much as it pained me to call some shrink, I knew that's the first thing Amber would ask me. I'd never make it to the date invite without passing that first hurdle.

The phone number sent me to the recovery group receptionist at Amber's church. She scheduled me for the next group meeting under the name Harry and recommended a website with additional resources. The receptionist was very helpful and sincere but completely useless for my drug-free, demon-filled life.

Now that I had an appointment on the calendar, I hoped Amber would give me a chance to explain things. I spent a few minutes cleaning myself up. Getting thrown around my apartment by Trench had left me looking a little frayed.

The moment I set foot out of my apartment, I spotted Amber and Heath arriving at her door down the hall. Luckily, they were already facing her apartment door and didn't see me. They appeared to be fresh from a Starbucks run because they both held large coffees. Or, in Heath's case, probably an organic, sustainable, free-trade, sugar-free, chai latte with soy milk. He had his guitar slung across his back, like a musical gypsy, waiting to cast more love-song spells on Amber.

The truth of the scene before me was unavoidable. They'd spent the afternoon together in her hour of need. Heath had been her shoulder to cry on. Her support system. Her soul searching companion.

The battle was over. He'd won.

CHAPTER 25

❖

Amber mumbled something to Heath before disappearing into her apartment and closing the door behind her. Heath stood there for a moment, adjusting his guitar strap. He turned and spotted me standing frozen outside my apartment.

He gave a head tilt my way. "Hey, bro."

"Hey." My shoulders slouched as defeat settled deep in my gut. The situation was clear. He'd become her comforter in a time of trouble, and I was the weird druggie next door.

There wasn't much left for me to do at that point but face the music and talk to my nemesis. I joined Heath outside Amber's apartment door.

"Rough day, huh?" I said.

He nodded. "She's having a hard time with things. Probably just needs some time alone."

Translation: I'm her shoulder to cry on now. You're nothing. Get lost.

"Yeah." My head dropped. My eyes made a lazy sweep of the faded yellow linoleum flooring of the hallway. Dust and scraps of paper outlined the edges of the hall and gathered in small piles in shadowy corners. Didn't they ever clean in here?

"The kitchen's done." Heath smoothed back an errant strand of his long hair. "Gonna have to close down."

"What?" It was like hearing a death sentence. It didn't seem real. "Didn't they have insurance or anything?"

"Yeah. Not enough. They had code violations and what not." Heath shrugged. "Insurance only covers part of the rebuild. Everything adds up to major bucks. They just can't swing it."

My stomach churned with a feeling of helplessness against the injustice of it all. It angered me how Heath was just taking everything in stride. "Well, we better do something. Get some churches together. Make some calls. Maybe one of those online fund raising things."

Heath pursed his lips, looking toward the stairway as if I was holding him up. "I don't think so, man. I already posted something on my YouTube channel. Not much response. Sometimes the writing's on the wall, you know? You just gotta flow with it."

"There's gotta be something we can do." The more he pronounced defeat, the more I was determined to change things. I was self-aware enough to realize part of my motivation was to argue against anything my rival to Amber's heart said, but deep down I knew it was much more. There were bigger things at stake here. Solas admitted as much. As crazy as it seemed, that humble little soup kitchen played a big part in the future of my city. I wasn't just going to stand by and watch it fall. "We have to at least try."

"I get it, man." He gave a lazy grin. "You're a new volunteer, and you're all fired up. I've been there. But I've traveled all over the world." He made a sweeping motion around the cramped hallway as if a giant atlas covered the walls. "I've been part of lots of movements and charities. There's always an energy about them. It's either surging or dying out. Sad to say, this one's dying, and it's time to let go. You have to flow with the momentum of the universe." He put a hand on my shoulder. "Better to use your strength for something with positive energy."

"You can't just bail when something's not going smooth," I said. "Sometimes you gotta stand your ground."

"Hey, follow your passion, bro. It's all good. Either way, I got a plane to catch." He jerked a thumb toward the stairway.

"Wait. Now?"

"Yep. Just nabbed a brand new video sponsor. They want surf footage in Samoa. The place is unreal." A broad smile covered his face. "Just spoke with their rep today. She said it's all expenses paid, but they're in a time crunch. Gotta happen now. Talk about timing. That's the kind of good energy I'm talking about. You gotta follow where it leads."

"Hold on." My sixth sense started buzzing. "This sponsor just called you out of the blue?"

"Pretty much."

"What's the rep's name?"

"Solas. Why?"

An eerie shiver swept over me. I grabbed him by the shoulders. "Listen, man. You can't go. I know it sounds crazy, but someone's trying to shut down the kitchen. She's trying to get us out of the way."

He smirked and raised his eyebrows like I was speaking gibberish. "She? As in, my new sponsor?"

"Yes. I know her. She runs drugs all over the city. She's got connections and money and power like you wouldn't believe. She'll get rid of anyone fighting for the kitchen. Including you."

He put up his hands. "Dude, you're trippin.' I told you to call that doctor, man. I've had bros go through this same paranoia stage."

"I'm clean," I said. "Trust me. Even if you think I'm crazy, what would be the harm in delaying the trip a little? Just stay and help us fight this thing. If it still fails, at least we did what we could."

Only a few moments ago my dream would be for Heath to tell me he was flying out of my life. But not like this. If any resistance was to be attempted, we needed everyone we could get to help. Even this vegan version of Thor trying to steal my girl.

"Hey, it's all good," Heath slapped my shoulder. "If you want to fight, fight. I don't like how things went down either. But first, you should call that doctor. Seriously."

"I called him. I already set up an appointment," I said. "Just stick around and help us."

"Can't do it, man." He cast a look back at Amber's door, pausing for a few moments. "Hate to end with Amber like this. I thought things with us might start up again, but, you know ... bad momentum." He sighed. "Well, it is what it is. See ya." And just like that he turned and headed down the stairs.

Only a few moments ago I would've celebrated watching Heath leave. But knowing that Solas was orchestrating this takeover changed everything. Heath was just one more unwitting obstacle she'd removed, putting more pressure on me and anyone else that stood against her.

I turned to Amber's door and poised to knock. What could I say to fix things? Would she even want to talk to me? I took a deep breath and knocked.

"Come on in." Amber called from inside.

I entered to find her putting clothes in a suitcase.

She looked up and her eyebrows raised. "Oh. Hey, Chris. I thought it was Heath."

"Yeah." I motioned behind me. "He just left. He filled me in on the kitchen."

Her face tightened like she was about to cry. I could tell

by her reddened eyes she'd probably been doing a lot of that already. Amber nodded and looked back at the suitcase, continuing to pack.

"Going somewhere?" I said.

"My mom's." She sniffed. "She lives over by the traffic circle. I really need her right now. I'm crashing at her place for a few days."

"Listen, Amber," I said. "I'm really sorry about everything."

"Yeah." Her arms dropped to her sides as she stared off in the distance. "Me too."

"I understand if you don't want to talk right now," I said. "I just wanted to stop by. Make sure you're okay."

She gave a tight smile. "Thanks."

"And I'm up for whatever to get the kitchen back up and running."

She stopped and looked back at me, her brows tightening. "What do you mean?"

"You know," I said. "Get some churches together, start a donation page online, whatever."

Her face softened. "Really? I mean, I want to, but we'd probably be the only ones. Everyone seems to think it's a lost cause."

I waved a dismissive hand. "Eh. That's just what losers say."

She chuckled. "Are you messing with me right now?"

She was warming up to me, so I joined her at the other side of her suitcase. "No. I'm in until the coroner declares this thing dead." I put out my hand. "Till the end?"

A lopsided smile animated her face like she was puzzled and amused at the same time. "You realize we don't have any money, right? Reality check. We need tens of thousands of dollars."

I moved my hand closer. "Come on, don't leave me hanging. I can't save this kitchen alone."

She grinned and shook my hand. "Okay, weirdo. This doesn't really change anything, you know. It's gonna take more than a few local churches pitching in. We've already reached out to several. They can spare a few hundred, maybe a few thousand if we're lucky. It's not enough. Unless you have a rich grandfather you haven't told me about, we need a miracle."

A beautiful thought suddenly hit me. Something Steve said about the art exhibit tonight sprang into memory like a golden lifeline.

"Hm," I rubbed my chin. "I wonder where a bunch of rich people would hang out tonight?" I spoke in theatrical tones. "You know, the type that would buy splatters of paint on canvas for a million dollars?"

She put her hands on her hips in a playful manner. "I'm listening."

I locked eyes with her. "Steve got accepted in an art exhibit tonight. Lots of people with lots of money."

A mischievous grin spread across her face. "Where and when?"

CHAPTER 26

Now that the cool breeze of rain-soaked air flowed through the windows, my apartment actually felt normal again.

Amber left to go to her mom's house until it was time for the exhibit. Unfortunately, this gave me plenty of alone time to freak out about my situation.

Solas's warning still echoed in my head. If I got involved, she would try to stop me. Even though my last sight of her was as a column of smoke fleeing my apartment, I knew the victory was short lived. To say she was crafty was like saying The Hulk had a temper. She had money and people at her beck and call. People like Trench who could easily make me sorry I'd gone against her. But why me? Why did it matter what I did? It was a strange thought that a demon would pay attention to a nobody like me. Unless, of course, I could do something to change things.

There was an hour left before I had to go. I was starving. Why did I commit to a fast? If there was ever a time to indulge in some stress eating it was now. I went to the kitchen and opened the fridge. A wave of expired sandwich meats hit me. I had to turn my head just to endure it. Apparently our econo fridge was the latest casualty of the broken apartment heater. Maybe it was a blessing in disguise. At least the temptation to break my fast was gone.

As long as my fast was still in effect, I decided to go full tilt and take Steve's advice. I shut off my phone, read scripture and prayed. I paid special attention to verses about demons and how the apostles dealt with them. As the minutes ticked by, a real sense of peace and confidence filled me. Aside from my conversion about four years ago, it was probably the most intense spiritual moment of my life.

After a quick shower, I threw on my one and only suit. The Armani I got from Solas. After all that had happened I was tempted to burn it. Can bad demon mojo linger in a suit? Just to be safe, I prayed over the suit, which felt really strange, then put it on.

By seven fifteen the rain stopped. Another lucky break. I fired up the motorcycle and revved the engine. There was a new found confidence running through me. I was on my way to the first official date with Amber, and I was riding a motorcycle in a suit at night which was very James Bond.

I wove through the rain slicked streets of Long Beach, my tires flicking streams of water at anyone who followed too close. Night in the city was like a photographic negative of daily life. Trees, blue sky and bright colors gave way to the yellow glow of street lights and storefront signs set against a charcoal backdrop.

I breathed deep and let the crisp air fill my lungs. The rain drove the smog of the city away, offering a glimpse into the respiratory life of healthy mountain people. Temple Avenue offered little resistance in the form of traffic. The occasional compact car was easy enough to weave around on my way toward Signal Hill.

A red traffic light at Anaheim Street killed my carefree mood, bringing me to an abrupt stop at the crosswalk. As I stared up at the glowing red of the light, I imagined Amber answering the door in a sequined red gown.

A car pulled up next to me with the windows down and stereo blasting. The harsh sounds of an over-the-top double bass pedal and screechy guitar-driven metal band drove away my vision of Amber. Why did people do this? How desperate for attention were they?

I looked over, hoping the darkened visor of my black helmet would give me an edge of intimidation. The guys inside the car looked like an ad for thug life. Blue lights from their dashboard lit up tattoo-ridden arms, strengthened with considerable gym mileage. Even though they wore wraparound shades, I could tell they were staring right at me.

That's when I noticed several horrible things at once. The thug in the passenger seat was Trench. The big guy that worked for Solas. Worse yet, the car was a grey El Camino.

For a fleeting moment I thought my helmet would hide my identity. That hope died as soon as Trench pointed and grinned at me. It was one of those grins exclusive to huge thugs that communicates that at any second they could destroy you.

Time to bolt. The light was still solid red. I was hedged in with cars on either side of me. I looked back at Trench. He was sliding something out of his inner jacket pocket. I spied the dead grey metal of a pistol grip in his hand. My adrenaline spiked. Cross traffic was sparse. I had to risk it.

My back tire spun on the slick road as I cranked the throttle. The bike fishtailed for a frightening moment before regaining traction. I shot into the intersection as fast as I could accelerate. An oncoming car blew his horn in protest, but I was already clear. I made it through the intersection without incident.

A powerful sounding engine revved and tires squealed

behind me. I craned my neck. The El Camino was pursuing. I had a good lead, but it wouldn't last. Motorcycles have the edge off the line, but a car with an engine like the one pursuing me would close the gap fast.

I raced through the gears of the motorcycle, gaining speed and praying for green lights. If only a cop could see us and step in, I'd gladly accept a speeding ticket.

The growl of the El Camino drew near. I wove around a beige pickup hoping to gain some ground. Unfortunately, the street traffic was light, and the thugs continued to gain.

My side mirror granted a frightening view of the car closing on me. Trench leaned out of the passenger window, his pistol extended in my direction. A primal sense of terror screamed within me. I was about to get shot.

Orizaba Park was on my right. A modest park with shady trees for picnics and a playground. A memory flashed through my mind of climbing the jungle gym as a kid. Just the thought of a place that felt safe at one time in my life urged me off the road.

I leaned into a treacherous turn. My back tire felt like it might give at any moment. Luck, God, Finch or maybe all three were with me as the bike held fast and hit the sidewalk entry at the perfect second to usher me safely onto the grass.

Tires skidded to a stop behind me. I headed further into the park, snaking through the dark trees. Just as I was feeling lucky for a well-timed dodge into the park, gunshots rang out. My body locked up at the fateful sound.

A chunk of bark blew off a tree just as I passed. Half a foot better aim and my head would have felt the blast instead. Another shot lifted a patch of grass just ahead. I weaved the bike through the park. A moving target was harder to hit. Another shot rang out, and I felt impact.

I took in a sharp gasp of air, my hands locking tight on the grips. For a split second I thought I'd been shot. A wave of relief went through me when I realized it wasn't me but the bike that got hit. I felt extremely lucky until the bike lurched toward the playground. The tire was out of whack and the steering was off. I cranked the handlebars in the right direction, but the bike wasn't responding. He must've shot out a tire. The bike surged into the woodchips of the playground. A glint from the metal chains of the swing set caught my eye. I was headed right for it.

I braked. Chains shook violently. I flew over the handlebars and braced for impact. I hit the sidewalk, just missing a park bench, and skipped onto the grass. There were several painful moments of tumbling and sliding through the rain-soaked grass before I came to a stop.

As I lay there struggling to catch my breath, tires pealed out, and the deep roar of the El Camino headed off into the night.

Any day you found yourself not leaking blood after being shot at was a good day. Sure, my Armani was torn and grass stained, mud streaks painted my body up and down, and my motorcycle was twisted up in swing set chains, but I was alive. As far as I could tell, there were no broken bones, and I was free of bullet holes, so I couldn't complain.

I removed my helmet and tried my best to clean off the suit. Between the mud and grass stains I looked pretty sad. To top it all off, one of my shoes was gone. After searching the surrounding area I came up empty. Without any options, I resigned to continue forward on one shoe and one wet sock.

My next challenge was detangling the swing chain wrapped around my bike. Turned out the back tire was blown out. It would be a costly repair, but better a bullet in the tire than in me.

As I freed my bike from the swing, an eerie sensation prickled my skin. It was the feeling I wasn't alone. My attention broke from the chains, and I scanned the vacant park.

Empty playground equipment squeaked as a cold wind

stirred the woodchips beneath it. What was it about playgrounds that made them seem so happy in the sunlight and so creepy at night?

Another gust of cold wind animated the branches of nearby trees. The rustle of the leaves sounded unnervingly like whispers.

The trees of the park weren't part of a new city project. They'd been there for decades, and the city built the park around them as generations came and went. The thick boughs of southern magnolias created a dark canopy overhead, and the cascading branches of Chinese elms felt like nets about to fall. Along with meager park lighting and the waning moon, the trees drenched me in shadows.

The darkest shadows near the base of the trees seemed to coalesce and shift. There was also movement in the upper darkness of the branches overhead. I begged my mind to believe I was seeing squirrels, but my instincts screamed that something far more sinister was present.

A strong urge grew within me to run. The desire was more than primal, the way I'd feel if a bear was preparing to chase me down. This impulse was a deeper, supernatural fear. The same sense that awoke when Solas transformed into smoky blackness.

I chanced another look into the boughs of a towering tree. That's when I saw them. Dozens of eyes looking down on me. Eyes with a faint glow like a dying star. The faint light revealed dark forms that resembled humans on the brink of starvation. The outline of rib cages and skulls showed under a thin covering of corpse-like skin. No, not skin. Something fluid. A grey substance that flowed around and through them.

These beings moved down the trees in unison, descending on my position.

For several moments it was hard to breath or even move. Frigid air, like a blanket of frost, settled on the park. Any confidence

I'd gained from purging my apartment of Solas seemed to fly out of me. I felt powerless. There were simply too many of these creatures.

My hands fumbled to free the remaining coil of chain from the bike tire. I was shaking so hard it was difficult to move correctly.

Ghastly moans sounded not more than a dozen feet away. The emaciated demons gathered at the trunk of the nearest tree, their ghostly white eyes fixed in my direction. They moved toward me, their bodies rising and falling into the earth as though some unseen tide pushed them forward.

The swing chain came loose and my bike was free. I heaved at the handlebars with panic-driven strength. The bike rolled onto the sidewalk and in a few seconds I was practically running. Had my mind been clearer, I would've just left the bike for dead and fled the demonic scene. But at that moment, the bike was my friend, and I couldn't abandon it.

Otherworldly voices called out behind me. There were cries of agony, hate filled threats, and desperate pleas for help all mixed into a frightening symphony. Even at my fear-driven pace, I felt them close behind, reaching for me.

CHAPTER 27

I dared not look back as I gained Temple Avenue and navigated into the bike lane. The unearthly moans of the demon swarm grew closer. My shoulders were tensed, expecting at any moment to feel the spectral grasp of demon claws around my neck.

Bright headlights shone from behind me. My heart leapt at the thought of another living, breathing human close by. I chanced a look over my shoulder. The vehicle was a huge, black stretch Hummer. The headlights illuminated the street all around.

At that moment I realized the voices were gone. The demons were nowhere in sight.

The stretch Hummer limo slowed to a stop right beside me. The tinted passenger-side window rolled down. The interior was darkened. The silhouette of a chauffeur in a black suit and cap leaned over from the driver seat.

"You okay?" he said.

I gave another look around to make sure the demons

where gone. All clear. I took a deep breath, my heart slowing down to a normal rhythm again.

"Yeah," I said, through heavy breaths.

"Looks like you took a bad spill," he said.

Now that I was free of the supernatural, my normal precautions came rushing forward. Who was this guy? Was he really being helpful or was something bad about to go down? Long Beach at night wasn't all peaches and cream.

"I'm fine." I gripped the handlebars, preparing to dive behind the bike if he had a weapon. Call me paranoid but with all I'd been through, I wasn't taking chances. "Cops should be here any second." I had no idea if the police were coming, but if this guy was bad news, I wanted to scare him away.

"Well," he said, "any accident you can walk away from is a good one, right?"

"Yep. Luck was on my side."

"Luck ... Or providence?" The chauffeur turned on the interior light. Finch, dressed as a limo driver, sat behind the wheel. He smiled. "Need a lift?"

Relief washed over me. "Finch! Man am I glad to see you!"

He tipped his cap. "At your service."

My mind quickly jumped from relief to frustration. I'd gone through the horrors of the day on my own. It sure would've been nice to have an angel step in to lend a hand.

"Where have you been?" I spread my hands in frustration, nearly dropping the bike with the effort.

Finch exited the stretch Hummer and walked toward me. "Busy. Lots to do in the spiritual realm. Here, I'll take that." He grabbed the handlebars, motioning with his hand for me to step back as if he was shooing an animal. "Why'd you buy a motorcycle in the first place? Death wish?" He shook his head and walked the bike to the back of the limo.

"That bike saved me," I said. "Unlike you. A pack of demons just tried to eat me!"

"Pfft." Finch gave a dismissive wave. "They're not zombies."

"Whatever. They were about to do something horrible. Aren't you supposed to be guarding me? Solas almost killed me tonight too. Where were you when she turned my room into the North Pole?"

He opened the back of the limo and chuckled. "Heard about that. I warned you to stay away from her. Nice job on the cast out though." He looked over and grinned. "My friend Sevultan saw the whole thing. Said you brought the power, JC style."

"Yeah, I guess. I'm just lucky I didn't get sledgehammered."

He shook his head. "Again, luck had nothing to do with it. Can I get a hand over here?"

I moved toward him and grabbed the other side of the bike, and together we lifted it into the back of the limo. Finch grunted as he heaved the bike off the ground.

"Why don't you just snap your fingers and make the bike appear inside?"

"I like to get my hands dirty. Keeps me in touch with the frailties of the human condition."

"Well, can you sprinkle some angel magic on it and fix my tire? And while you're at it,"—I motioned to my grass and mud stained suit—"how 'bout a fresh set of clothes? And shoes?"

"What am I? Your fairy godmother?" Finch closed up the back and latched it. "You want some glass slippers, too?" He laughed and headed for the driver's seat.

I sighed and joined him in the Hummer. At least I wouldn't have to push my bike.

Finch headed down the street, the limo radio blasting A-ha's "Take On Me." He sang along with the falsetto in perfect pitch, drumming his hands on the steering wheel to the beat.

I reached over and shut off the radio. "What are you doing?"

He frowned at me. "Hey, I was listening to that."

"Demons are after me!" I stabbed at my chest with both hands to emphasize my dire predicament. "Demons! Dark supernatural creatures crawling out of trees to get me. I've got major problems here, and you want to listen to some goofy eighties song?"

Finch furrowed his brow and turned to me, taking his hands off the wheel. "First of all,"—he started counting off on his fingers—"demons are always creeping around trying to mess with things. Just because you're suddenly aware of them doesn't mean you're in a worse situation..."

The limo began to drift into the wrong side of the street. My eyes widened, and I made frantic motions to oncoming traffic. Finch gave a casual wave, and the steering wheel took on a life of it's own, correcting our course.

"Second,"—Finch counted off another finger—"the same power you called upon to cast out Solas is available twenty-four / seven. You're the one that choose not to use it. And third, as far as Earth music goes, that song rules. Trust me on this, I've heard a lot of songs over the centuries."

"Whatever, look, I'm freaking out okay," I said. "Maybe this all seems like a typical Sunday night to you, but I'm in uncharted territory. I need help!"

Finch scratched at his chin, a pensive expression on his face. "Hm, true ... You see? This is why I'm not on regular assignment. Lack of bedside manner and all that. Now Gabriel, he's a people person. Chances are, he'd be serving you a cup of warm tea and toast right now. Michael on the other hand—"

"Okay, I get it. You're the angel on probation I'm stuck with. Just help me out here."

He put a hand over his heart and stuck out his lower lip. "I'm not going to pretend that didn't hurt." He looked skyward as if lost in thought. "I think I'm starting to understand why we were put together."

"Hello?" I waved to get his attention.

Finch snapped out of it. "Yes, right. Let me start with this. You're on the right track. Otherwise, they'd leave you alone. You're obviously playing a critical part in all this."

"Solas said something about the soup kitchen being a domino," I said. "That if it fails, it would start a of chain of events."

Finch nodded. "The 'ripples in the lake' principle."

"So, is this like, with everything?" I said. "When I don't do something good, bad things snowball?"

"Well, it's not like if you eat too many donuts innocent children die. It's not that simple. Let's just say, if you avoid doing the good you're called to do, the results could compound negatively. Conversely, if you pursue the good, positive results could multiply. People tend to think of choices as isolated events. They don't realize that small things left unchecked can initiate big issues down the road."

I sat back in my seat, letting the thought sink in. How many noble pursuits had I let slip by in life while I sat on the sidelines? Even worse, what negative fires had I lit the match to while pursuing my own selfish desires?

As terrifying as my current situation was, I couldn't back out now from fighting for the soup kitchen. It was time to go all in and let the chips fall where they may.

"Okay," I said. "I'm ready for this. You're with me, right?"

"That's the spirit." Finch pumped his fist. "Just remember, I can only intervene where allowed. If things get ugly and you end up in heaven tonight, it's not because I took a nap or anything."

"Wait, what?" I stared at him. "Heaven? You mean I might die?"

He nodded. "Wasn't that clear?"

"No! I thought you were supposed to protect me?"

"You just got shot at, crashed into playground equipment

at full speed on one of the most dangerous forms of transportation available, and you only have minor scrapes and bruises. Trust me, there's been intervention. I'm just saying, with any endeavor, there's a chance of injury or death. No one is promised tomorrow."

The thought of dying to keep a soup kitchen open never occurred to me. Now that death was on the table, my desire for self preservation was screaming at me to bail on the whole endeavor.

"That doesn't even make sense," I said. "I'm trying to do something good here. That's my reward? Death? How would that help anything?"

"Dying for a cause can be a big motivator," Finch said. "It often wakes those into action who would otherwise sit still."

I slumped back in my seat, my head sinking into the cushioned head rest. "I don't believe this."

Finch patted me on the shoulder. "There, there now. I never said it was going to happen. Just that it might. Worse case scenario, I'll see you in the afterlife. You'll love it. I'll show you around. Give you harp lessons."

I gave him a dark look.

"Kidding," he said. "I don't play the harp. Bad stereotype. I do, however, play a klensprix. It's like a guitar only with fifty strings. And the spectrum of perceivable sound is about five thousand times that of earth, so you're gonna be blown away when I jam." He looked up as if something just occurred to him. "Hey, maybe I'll write a song about all this."

A ring sounded near the parking brake. His giant, brick-sized phone sat on it's antique dock between us.

Finch grabbed the phone. "Hello? Now? Okay, if you say so." He hung up. "Duty calls. Gotta go."

"You're leaving me?"

"Don't worry, I'll be back. We're a team, remember?" He put up a hand for a high five.

I scowled at him.

He frowned and slowly lowered his hand. "Look, we're working different angles of the same project, okay? Tapestry-of-events principle and all that."

"I have no idea what you're talking about," I said. "All I know is I need to pick up Amber at her mom's and get to an art exhibit so we can—"

"Yes, I'm well aware. No time to waste. Let's get you to the ball, Cinderella." He snapped his fingers and there was a bright flash of light.

CHAPTER 28

The next thing I knew, I was standing on a porch at the front door of a house I didn't recognize. My suit was clean and pressed as though straight from a dry cleaner. A shiny, new pair of Oxfords were on my feet. One problem—the shoes were fashioned from a clear plastic material. They looked as if they were made of glass. You could see straight through to my black, pinstripe socks. Apparently this was Finch's idea of a joke.

The front door opened, and Amber stood in the doorframe. She rocked a white, off-the-shoulder evening gown that made me feel like I was headed to prom. She looked incredible.

Her eyebrows raised as she checked out my suit. "You clean up nice."

"Thanks," I said. "You look amazing. Like a princess."

"Ugh." She winced.

"Sorry. I mean like a queen."

Her head tilted in a side-to-side rhythm as if deciding the merit of the compliment.

"Like a goddess," I tried.

Amber chuckled. "Too far." She looked behind me. "What happened to your bike?"

I craned my neck back. My bike laid on its side across her front lawn as if it had just slid into home plate. The back tire was still blown out. Apparently bike repair was a step beyond Finch's willing scope of power.

"Let's just say I almost died getting here."

"Just for the chance to take me out, huh?"

"You're worth it."

Amber smirked. "Just because you're looking all suave, don't think you can sweet talk me." She reached back and grabbed a set of keys from the entry table. "Come on, we'll take my car."

Soon we were in her compact coupe headed toward Signal Hill. The artificial vanilla scent from the car mixed with her floral perfume in the best possible combination. I decided if I did end up in heaven tonight, I'd request a bottle of this aroma.

"Chris?" Amber had a tentative tone in her voice.

"Yeah?" I braced for impact.

"I know it's not really fair of me to ask, but did you call that doctor?"

"Yep. Signed up for the group meeting next week." If I live to see next week, of course.

She smiled. "I've heard great things about Dr. Plinse."

"I totally get your concern. I was rambling this morning. I probably sounded crazy or high or something. Bottom line is, I don't do drugs. I don't even like wine. Just a beer now and then. But I'm willing to go to the meeting if it'll put your mind at ease."

As a traffic light turned red, Amber slowed to a stop. She looked at me for several moments, a warm smile hanging on her lips. Her caramel-colored hair wound around her neck and draped over her bare shoulder. The street light overhead fell softly across her warm brown eyes and full lips. I wanted to remember that moment forever.

"Forget what I said." She shook her head. "Don't go to the meeting."

"Really?" I said.

She nodded. "It's weird. Somehow I know I can trust you. There's something different about you lately. When I first met you, I thought you were ... well, anyway, I'm really glad I got to know you better."

Even though not so subtle insults about my first impressions were clear, I didn't mind. She was probably right. Up until about a week ago, my life was a little confused. It was amazing how fast things had focused. Being with someone I really cared about at that moment, working together for something bigger than myself, something of supernatural importance, was the meaning my life had been lacking. Of course, things had become a thousand times more dangerous in the process, but hey, there's always a trade off.

"I called Gwen," Amber said. "Told her what we're trying to do."

"Yeah? What'd she say?"

"Well, in her fifteen years of heading up Caring Tables, she says it's the worst spot they've been in and wanted to tell us *thank you* for what we're trying to do."

I nodded. "Cool."

"She also said it's a long shot and not to get our hopes up." Amber gave a wry grin. "She's got a heart of gold, but she's a realist."

"All the more reason to shock her when we snag a big donation tonight," I said.

"I love your blind determination. I tell you, this whole thing has really cleared up some things." She looked at me intently. "You stepped up when everyone else wanted to give in. Heath bailed without a second thought. I guess I should've known."

"Yeah, what a loser," I joked.

She gave me a playful punch. "He's a good guy ... just not the right guy. He's always looking for the next thrill. That's not what I want out of life. I want to stay close to my community. Help out where I can."

"I tell you what you need," I pointed at my chest. "A guy like me."

She gave a sidelong glance. "Is that right?"

"Think about it. After a long day, you come back to your apartment and don't want to be alone, who can you turn to for good conversation or a shoulder to cry on?"

"Steve?" she said.

I frowned. "That's messed up."

She grinned. "Let's just say, if tonight goes well, a goodnight kiss isn't out of the question."

"Now you're talking."

We drove for a few moments in silence, an excitement running through me at the thought of a new relationship with this amazing woman.

It took only minutes to reach Signal Hill. Amber's cough-drop shaped coupe climbed the steep streets, the houses growing taller and more luxurious the higher we went. We passed Hilltop Park and followed the surrounding street to a gated community called Pinnacle Estates. We punched in the code Steve texted me and an automatic iron-rod gate swung open, granting us entry.

We turned down a row of multimillion dollar homes on Starry Lane and found our destination. A three-level modern-style mansion with balconies on the upper levels to capitalize on the hill top view. We got out, our heads lifted high to admire the house.

Amber whistled. "Not bad."

"I've seen better," I said.

She smirked and pulled my hand forward. "Come on, you big goon."

The house was stunning. The entryway was a beautiful assault of exotic hardwood flooring, ornate carvings, and imported furniture. Small tables held shiny silver antiques like offerings to the gods. My guess was they were never touched except by maids who polished them on cleaning day.

Dozens of well-dressed guests strolled through the house, admiring the surroundings or sharing hushed comments. Champaign glasses clinked somewhere nearby.

"What a nightmare," I said.

"Well, this is it." She smoothed her dress. "Our last chance to save Caring Tables. There's probably a philanthropist or two around here. Let's find them."

I nodded, suddenly feeling the weight of the task ahead of us. We needed tens of thousands of dollars. Would some random stranger actually agree to such a hefty donation. "Where do we start?"

She scanned the suits and evening gowns milling around us. "We need to work the crowd." She pointed to the sprawling living area to her left. "I'll take the left wing, you get right. Deal?"

"We're splitting up?"

"There's a lot of ground to cover." Amber leaned in and kissed my cheek. Lights sparkled from the spiraling chandelier overhead making her eyes look alive with magic. "This is our big chance."

With a whirl of her dress she was off. I stood there for a moment, unsure what to do next. How did one find a philanthropist? It's not like they had badges. Was I just supposed to introduce myself to strangers and ask for money? Suddenly I was the homeless panhandler of the party.

"Chris!" Steve descended from a winding staircase. "You made it."

True to form, he wore jeans, a T-shirt, and a sport coat. If nothing else, it helped him stand out in the crowd as one of the artists. Julie clung to his arm sporting a shimmering blue gown. She gazed at him like a proud girlfriend.

Steve glanced down at my feet and smirked. "Nice shoes, man."

"They were a gift." I turned to his date, anxious to get the attention off my feet. "Hey, Julie."

"Hi, Chris." She smiled. "Isn't this great?"

"Yeah. Fancy."

Steve looked around. "Amber couldn't make it, huh?"

"She's here. She's hunting philanthropists."

He raised his brow.

"A fire took out the soup kitchen," I said. "She's trying to get funding to save it."

He nodded. "Wow. Good for her. If I meet any, I'll send them her way."

Julie patted his shoulder. "You should show Chris your display. I'll get some drinks."

He squeezed her hand. "Thanks."

"Have fun." She smiled at Steve and headed off.

I raised my eyebrows. "She is totally into you tonight."

Steve held up his hands. "Don't jinx it." He studied me a moment. "Listen, I know you're going through stuff. I can take a break from my exhibit if you need to talk."

"Thanks, man." He had no idea how much that meant at this crazy moment in my life.

A server in a tux came by with a silver tray of hors d'oeuvres. A wave of aromas straight from heavens kitchen engulfed me.

"Gentlemen?" The server lowered the tray toward us. A bewitching array of bite-sized treats spread out before me.

"Thanks." Steve snatched up several. "Chris, you gotta try these." He turned to the server. "What do you call them again?"

"Lobster tartlets with bacon and fresh avocado," the server said.

My hand seemed to lift and hover over the tartlets of it's own accord. My mouth filled with saliva. I hesitated. Had I come this far to indulge now?

"What's wrong?" Steve broke my food haze.

"Um..." My eyes were still glued on the tartlets. "I'm kind of fasting right now."

"Really?" Steve chuckled. "Since when do you fast?"

"Since today." I picked up one of the tartlets. There was a shimmering glow of grease on the golden crust. I could smell the luscious bacon inside.

"Gimme that." Steve grabbed the tartlet from my hand. "Thanks, we're all set." He directed the server away from us.

I stared after the departing silver tray as if watching an old friend leave town.

"Stay strong, man." Steve popped the tartlet in his mouth. "These aren't worth it."

I glared at him. "Easy for you to say."

"I'll take you to breakfast tomorrow," he said with a full mouth. "My treat."

"Deal." I watched the smooth flow of the rich and powerful walking by. "So, do people actually buy art at this thing?"

A broad grin spread across his face. He handed me a check. "What do you think?"

The check was made out to Steve in the amount of seven thousand dollars.

"Seven thousand!" I said.

"Shh." Steve snatched the check and stuffed it back in his pocket. "Chill, man. You've gotta act like it's no big deal."

My mouth hung open. "Someone paid that much for your paintings?"

"Yeah, some producer that does reality TV. And that was just one painting," he said.

"What?" I exclaimed.

He gave an embarrassed look around. "Dude, you're making a scene."

"I'm sorry. That's ridiculous. Why am I not painting?"

He patted my shoulder. "Can you get it together?"

I put up my hands. "Okay, okay. Unbelievable. Good job."

Steve nodded. "Making rent won't be a problem for awhile."

"Yeah. Oh, and I have two grand to help out now."

He narrowed his eyes. "How?"

"My payment for deliveries. But don't worry, I'm done with all that. I'm moving on. I'm taking that comic book store job."

"There you go," he said. "Look at us. Two broke artists making money."

I spread out my hands. "I know, right?"

He grinned and waved me forward. "Come on, I'll show you my part of the exhibit. I still have three paintings left."

He took me upstairs to a round room with a grand piano as the centerpiece. Floor to ceiling windows on the far wall granted a breathtaking bird's eye view of the city lights at night.

"Check it out." Steve motioned to his three paintings that covered the non-windowed half of the room.

"Wow. Steve, this is incredible." I was genuinely impressed. Seeing his paintings displayed on the walls of a swanky mansion definitely made them look legit. Even though they were the exact same paintings that had gathered dust in our shabby apartment, I had to admit, my opinion of their worth was swayed by the venue.

A statuesque brunette entered the room behind us. A red dress cascaded down her trim frame. Fine, glittering jewelry told the story of a well-financed woman. She walked as though she were gliding and her every move had the casual grace of a finishing school valedictorian.

Steve turned to her. "Ms. Alcon. This is my friend, Chris."

She gave me a slight nod. "Hello, Chris."

"Hi," I said.

"This is her place. And her exhibit," Steve said. "She's the one that invited me to be part of it."

Ms. Alcon touched his shoulder lightly. "You deserve it. Your work is magnificent."

Steve gave a bashful look down. "Well, thank you. I'm honored to be here."

She turned to admire Steve's paintings. "Such emotion. The bleak struggle of humanity. I find his despair transformative." She turned to me. "Don't you?"

Steve's lips went thin as though holding back a laugh. He enjoyed seeing me put on the spot. Especially with something as out of my league as art critique.

I gave a studied look at the painting in front of me. The focal point was a small, luminous figure fleeing through a vortex of darkness. Steve definitely knew how to stick it to his creations.

"Indeed." I rubbed my chin thoughtfully. "His anguish is sublime."

Steve started coughing as if to mask laughter.

A thin man in a tux walked up to Ms. Alcon.

"Hello, Jenson," she said. "Are the guests enjoying themselves?"

He gave a slight bow. "Yes, ma'am. And your donation to the animal shelter was well received. Mr. Greenville wishes to express his deepest thanks."

She gave a subtle nod. "Thank you, Jenson. Please make sure everyone's drinks are refreshed."

Jenson gave another bow and walked out at a brisk pace. Steve and I exchanged a quick look. The same light bulb must've gone off in his head. As awkward as it was to ask anyone for money, how could I pass this up? Most of the people in my sphere of influence had to scrape together change for tacos.

"That was very generous," I said. "An art lover and a philanthropist, huh?"

Ms. Alcon gave a light shake of her head. "I've been blessed in this life. It's the least I can do."

"You know," I tried to speak casually. "I volunteer at a local soup kitchen. They try to improve the community just like you. Unfortunately, just today criminals hit their place. They set fire to the kitchen and shut it down."

She put a hand to her mouth. "That's terrible. Where did it happen?"

"Caring Tables." I said. "You know it?"

"Yes. They do marvelous work. Oh, what a shame."

I nodded. "We're trying to raise funds for repairs. My date tonight is actually one of their full time volunteers. We're hoping someone may be able to help. Every bit counts."

I tried to play it cool, but inside I was bracing for a backlash. Rich or not, who likes to get cornered for donations in their own home?

She gave a warm smile and touched my hand. "I'd love to help. Why don't you connect your date with my assistant, Jenson. Tell him to write a check for whatever is needed to reopen the kitchen."

"Really?" My brain stuck. Did she just offer to pay for all the expenses? "That's amazing ... Are you serious?"

She smiled. "Of course. Besides art, improving our community is a passion of mine."

"This is incredible," I said. "I'll go tell her right now."

"There's no rush," she said. "You haven't even had time to enjoy your friend's display."

"Oh, that's okay." I waved her off. "He's my roommate. I see his work all the time."

"Nonsense." She turned to Steve. "Would you mind connecting Jenson with Chris's date so they can work out the details."

"Yeah, of course." Steve said. "Thank you. This is really great of you."

"Please, it's nothing."

Steve smiled and hurried out of the room.

I felt like electricity was running through me. Amber would probably marry me after tonight.

"Wow," I said. "Honestly, this is more than I could've hoped for. Thank you from the bottom of my heart."

"It's the least I could do. After all"—she went back to admiring Steve's paintings—"I'm not actually going to give you any money."

I paused. "What?"

She smirked. "I'm going to write a generous check, delay payment for awhile, then decline it."

I waited a few moments for a punchline that never came. This woman was either vindictive or bats. Either way, my hopes were fading fast. "You're joking, right?"

She shook her head. "The soup kitchen will fall regardless. This is just entertainment while I wait. My false donation will raise hopes, then dash them to pieces." She chuckled. "I already have a construction crew scheduled to tear that wretched kitchen down to it's foundation. It's really just a question of when."

She turned to me, her body slowly transforming into Solas. My heart stopped. A chill crept over my skin.

"Hello, Chris." She winked. "Miss me?"

CHAPTER 29

※

I stood there speechless. A hollow sensation opened in my stomach as if I was about to be swallowed from the inside out. No matter where I turned, I was trapped in this supernatural fight. There was nowhere to hide. The lights in the room grew dim, and the temperature dropped.

"You can cast me away, but you can't stop me, Chris," Solas said. "Whatever you think you can accomplish, you're wrong. I influence who I want, and they do as I wish. I could show you the devoted sheep out there that have prayed and cried and sacrificed for years to keep my work from happening. It hasn't stopped me. The supernatural dam has burst, and the flood is already on it's way." She put her hand on my shoulder. A flash of cold shot down my arm and poured through my body. At once I seemed frozen in place.

"Come with me." She left the room and signaled me to follow with a flick of her finger.

A dark sensation urged me to follow. I resisted for a moment, and icy prickles formed across my back like a rough wall of ice pushing against me. The room temperature continued to drop. I wanted out of this cursed place.

I hurried from the room only to find Solas waiting for me. She'd turned back into the taller, brunette-haired Ms. Alcon. She leaned against the edge of an ornate, curved railing that overlooked the first floor. Two guys dressed in tuxes that could barely contained their bulky frames stood at attention beyond her, blocking the passage to the staircase. They looked like secret service standing guard. I did a double take realizing it was Trench and his thug partner from the El Camino. The tuxes covered their tattoos and gave them the appearance of high-priced security, but their faces conveyed their usual cold malevolence.

Solas motioned for me to come near. What could I do? I joined her at the railing. I felt like a doomed soldier with no cavalry.

Below, a few artists stood near their displays on the first floor, the guests walking by or stopping for a moment to admire their work.

"That's Jetta." Solas pointed to a young girl with pixie-cut purple hair and thick eyeliner. "Her real name is Ann." A trio of paintings with dark red streaks over crumbling walls of ruined civilizations hung behind her. Jetta wore a white faux-fur crop top and black leather pants, with bare feet. She obviously cared little for the dress code.

"You want an example of my influence?" Solas said. "Jetta went off course from my plans a few weeks ago."

"Off course?" I said.

"Her spirit was stirred. Her mother'd been praying for her." Solas grimaced. "The stirring was strong enough to move her to action. She almost bought a Bible. I diverted her thoughts enough to get her to go to church instead. Not ideal, of course, but better than going straight to the source."

Jetta sauntered up to a young guy in a suit who stopped by

her exhibit. She seemed so confident, even brash. She threw her head back and let out a bawdy laugh at something he said.

"Luckily, I already had good intel on a shaky local church I directed her to," Solas continued. "Plenty of gossips, hidden sins, and insecurities to work with. I convinced Jetta that spirituality was fine as long as it didn't change who she was. Of course, I used this thought to get her to church wearing suggestive clothing. Nothing scandalous mind you, just enough to get the judgmental types in a tizzy." Solas turned to me and smiled broadly. "By the time service was over, I'd stoked the fires of insecurity so that most of the women were already whispering about her. No one even reached out to welcome her. The pastor was the only one that even said hello. Of course, I had his wife give a snide remark on the drive home about flirting with girls half his age."

Solas placed her hands on the railing. She looked down at Jetta, a sneer animating her cheek. "After that morning, I made sure to remind her of all the sins of her past. Hammering home the same message given off by the gossips. She was unworthy. She didn't belong in church."

"No one is worthy," I broke in. "We're saved by grace."

"Grace." Solas practically snarled as she said the word. "I could tell you similar stories about all my artists. They're all under my thumb." She took out her phone and held the screen so I could see it. "Including you." A video feed of Harbor near Second Street played. The camera focused on a large yacht docked in a slip. The night mist was thick, but in the dusky harbor lights someone snuck onto the yacht holding a bright red present with a bow. That someone was me.

"Whoops." Solas said. "Look who's sneaking onto the mayor's boat in the middle of the night. And delivering a package filled with cocaine."

I turned on her. "You gave me that. That's your drugs."

She held up her free hand. "The only face on this video is

yours. I also have the testimony of the concierge at Silver Towers who you delivered drug money to. Not to mention several recently incarcerated drug dealers who will testify that you showed up at their house this morning to run drug deliveries."

"Your deliveries." I pointed at her. "I can testify as well. They know the name Ms. Callow. They've seen your face."

"Have they?" Her face transformed through several different identities in a matter of seconds. "I'm a figment of their imagination. A ghost. Do you really think I could be arrested?" She laughed.

I felt a growing weight on my shoulders. She held all the cards. Not only power and influence, but now she could blackmail me.

"So this is your game?" I said. "Get dirt on people? Accuse them of their past? Hold them down so they feel unworthy or afraid to do what's right?"

She gave a devilish smile. "It's true art. The greatest exhibit of all. Satan, the master artist himself, has perfected it to a science. It's kept humanity down for centuries. It's especially beautiful when people do it to each other. They do the work for us."

Everything was spiraling downward. There was nothing I could say to fix things. She had me cornered. At that moment I prayed a desperate prayer. In my state of distress, it wasn't much different from begging. I pleaded for supernatural help.

Psalm 23 jumped to the forefront of my thoughts. The words were so strong and clear I spoke them aloud. "The Lord is my shepherd, I shall not want. He makes me lie down in green pastures, He leads me beside quiet waters. He restores my soul..."

Solas frowned. Her face tightened. "Stop that."

Her reaction bolstered my efforts. I closed my eyes and continued. "He guides me in the paths of righteousness for His name's sake—"

"Stop!" Solas shrieked.

"Even though I walk through the valley of the shadow of death, I fear no evil, for You are with me—"

Strong hands gripped my arms and yanked me backward. I opened my eyes to find Trench and the other thug at either side of me, grasping my biceps in their meaty hands. Trench sent a sucker punch into my side. The wind was knocked out of me and sharp pain radiated across my rib cage. I collapsed like a puppet in their grasp.

"Take him to the roof." Solas pointed upward.

The thugs yanked me down the hallway. In addition to my prayers for deliverance, I threw in a request that my arms would stay attached to their sockets.

They pulled me through a side door and up a narrow flight of stairs. Trench kicked open a door, and the next thing I knew we were out in the night air on a rooftop patio. Stars blinked overhead, thin layers of clouds creeping across the sky. A Cheshire Cat-smile of a moon shone down as if gleefully watching my impending doom.

The thugs pulled me forward at a brisk pace, my feet dragging behind. The toes of my shoes drummed out a staccato rhythm as they rubbed across the spaces of the wooden deck. Cushy seating surrounded narrow cylinder-shaped tables with brightly lit fires as their centerpiece. An invisible-line swimming pool dominated the north end of the patio, underwater lights painting it a luminescent blue.

A dazzling geometric display of city lights rushed toward me as we closed on a brushed-metal railing.

The thugs spun me around and forced my back against the unforgiving metal. They pushed against my shoulders, causing my upper body to lean past the top rail. I craned my neck to see where I was headed. A three-story drop onto a field of rocks waited below.

The house was positioned at the edge of the hill. Only dirt

fields, sharp rocks, and mismatched clumps of trees populated the downward sloping hillside beyond. A few oil rigs sat dormant on isolated platforms in the distance. Remnants of the oil fields that once drove the local economy.

"How do you like the view?" Solas sauntered toward us, her visage transformed back to the supermodel blonde I first met.

"It sucks," I said.

She smiled. "Your defiance is empty. You're insignificant in my plans."

"Then why spend so much time on me?" I said. "You've gone to a lot of trouble to keep me distracted. Threatening me to stay away. If I'm insignificant, why all the effort?"

"You're right. Perhaps it's time to kill you." She glanced at Trench. The thugs pushed my shoulders further over the railing. My feet left the ground, and I teetered on the top rail.

"I was going to let you live, but I changed my mind," she said. "Oh, and your little girlfriend will die, too. I'll make sure it's nice and painful. And Steve, well, I'll string him along with his art for awhile, build his hopes up, then wreck him. I'll unleash my art critics on him. Make him feel like his lifelong pursuit is a sad failure. I'll spend years burning down his life, savoring every precious moment."

Something deep within me welled up. Something that had grown tired of responding to fear. A reckless sensation to grab hold of my faith and dive into this fight head first. If I was going to die tonight, I might as well go down swinging. I prayed a last prayer for mercy and deliverance.

"Maybe I should call on the power of Jesus," I said. "See if he wants to join the party."

A look of rage flashed on her face. Her teeth showed like a dog ready to attack. "I'll tear you apart!"

"That's in God's hands." I felt a strength surge within me. "I call on the power of Jesus to command you to leave this place."

A myriad of lights swirled around the rooftop as though stars had descended from the night sky. A rush of wind accompanied the lights, the current flowing around us like a building whirlwind.

Solas shrunk back and stumbled into one of the narrow tables with a center flame. There was a metallic crack, and the fire flashed brightly. The table toppled onto a nearby couch, and the cushions burst into flames. The thugs lessened their grip on my shoulders. My feet found solid ground once more.

The whirlwind around us gained intensity. The fire spread across the wood flooring, and the other seating areas went up in flame.

Solas cowered by the burning couch, her expression twisted into a snarl. She unleashed a string of profanities as the flames cast a devilish glow on her face. "I'll make you suffer. I'll kill everyone you care about!"

A bold confidence flooded through me. "Didn't I tell you to leave? By the power and authority of Jesus Christ, leave this place and never return!"

Her face shriveled as though decades of age had descended in only a moment. Her hair turned white, the silky appearance changing to a wiry mass. She shrieked and put her wrinkled arms up as if defending against physical attack.

The swirling wind grew, flooding the area with warmth. Lights danced within the currents like giant fireflies caught in the breeze. White hair whipped about Solas's face. She threw her head back and screamed as she dissipated in a cloud of grey dust that the whirlwind caught up.

I couldn't believe she was gone. All the terror and stress I'd been through as a result of letting her into my life had crumbled into fragments that the wind swept away. Was this really the end of her dark hold over me?

The fire spread quickly with the winds. Large sections of the roof burned brightly against the dark skies. The flames crackled and sent sparks spiraling upward in a column of black smoke.

The heat was unbearable. My skin felt as though it might burst into flame. I coughed as the smoke blew against me, gasping for the dwindling oxygen.

Trench and the other thug released me. They looked toward the stairway door, but before us was a wall of impenetrable flame. They took a few unsure steps and stopped. The other thug glanced at Trench, then bolted into the flames. Trench looked back at me. The flames illuminated his face. His eyes were wide. For the first time his expression was void of strength. He had the fearful gaze of a child.

He took off after the other thug, holding his arms over his face, and disappeared into the fire. Terrifying screams came from the flames. It was one of the worst sounds I'd ever heard. The screams continued for a few horrifying seconds, then went silent.

I looked over the railing. My only option was jumping. If I survived the fall, there'd be untold broken bones. It was either that or burn alive with the thugs.

As I gathered the courage to leap over the railing, the swirling winds washed over me. Through squinted eyes, I watched the winds cut a path through the flames and hold them at bay. The winds maintained a narrow path through the fire that lead right to the stairway door.

A gust of wind urged me forward. I ran through the building flames, my body covered in a layer of sweat. Using my shirt, I turned the hot metal doorknob and dashed down the stairway.

When I reached the second story bannister, the guests were already in a panic. People were screaming and running for safety. Grey smoke flooded into the house from the roof.

The double door entrance was a bottleneck of bodies pushing against each other to escape. I was just about to rush down the stairs and join the hysteric masses when I realized Steve's paintings still hung in the room nearby.

Without thinking, I rushed into the room. Grey smoke gathered on the ceiling and flowed like a stagnant breeze. With the few bits of fire safety I remembered from elementary school safety videos, I ducked low and breathed through my shirt. My eyes stung and watered like crazy. I yanked his three paintings off the wall and bolted out of there.

I coughed deep, sickly coughs on my way down the stairs. My head spun like I might pass out at any moment. I plunged into the crowd pressing through the doorway. Luckily the number of people had diminished a bit during my painting rescue.

After several panicked seconds of pushing and being squashed from multiple angles, I burst onto the front lawn, gasping with pleasure at the fresh, night air. I half-jogged, half-stumbled to the curb where I fell to my knees, dropping the paintings in the process.

CHAPTER 30

"Chris!" Amber rushed over, falling to her knees beside me. "Are you okay?"

I nodded, too busy coughing to respond.

Steve and Julie followed right behind Amber. "What happened?"

"He took in some smoke," Amber said. "Are the paramedics here yet?"

"I hear sirens," Julie said.

Sure enough, the escalating whine of sirens headed toward us. Within moments, a fire engine and an ambulance pulled up to the house.

"Are those my paintings?" Steve rushed to his paintings, lifting them off the lawn as if to make sure they were okay. "You saved my paintings?" Steve looked at me like I just transformed into an alien. "You charged through a burning building for these?"

"Yeah." I coughed. "You owe me big time."

He hugged me like a long lost brother. "They wouldn't let

anyone upstairs after the roof collapsed." Tears welled up in his eyes. "I thought these were lost. That was crazy of you to go back for them."

I shrugged. "What can I say? I'm a superhero."

Julie squeezed my arm. "Thank you, Chris."

The roof was now a giant bonfire. Fireman rushed forward, their heavily-booted feet clomping over the sidewalk. They pulled a thick hose into place, preparing to douse the blaze. The whole area was awash with heat and smoke.

Amber grabbed my face and turned it toward her. "You sure you're okay?"

"I think so," I said. "You?"

She smiled and nodded. "I hope everyone got out all right." She looked toward the flames. "I guess that generous donation is off the table now."

"Yeah," I said. "Pretty sure that donation was a false promise anyway."

Amber frowned. "I kind of got that feeling, too. Steve told me about it, but when we talked to her assistant, Jenson, he seemed really squirrelly about the whole thing."

"Yeah," I coughed. "Sorry."

She looked back toward the house, the reflection of flames dancing in her glossy eyes. "That's the second burning building I've been in today. This is the weirdest day ever."

She had no idea.

"I can't believe you got Steve's paintings," she said. "You know you can die from smoke inhalation, right?"

If she only knew how many times I almost died today.

A stout paramedic with a bushy red mustache hurried over to us. "Everyone okay over here?"

Amber pointed to me. "He breathed in a lot of smoke."

The paramedic set down his gear and began rifling through it. "If any of you have cars near the house, you'd better get them clear."

"Good idea," Steve grabbed my shoulder. "Listen, I got rent for awhile. Why don't you take that money you made and make your graphic novel happen. You finally have enough now to self-publish a quality comic."

"What?" I said. "No, I can't do that."

"I want you to do it. Serious."

"Man, that would be unbelievable. You sure?"

He smiled. "My mind is set. I'll see you back home."

Steve and Julie gathered his paintings and headed off.

"I'll swing the car around." Amber made a U-turn motion with her hand and hurried away.

The paramedic put an oxygen mask on me and started checking my vitals. I stared in shock at the beautiful mansion that was all but lost to the ascending flames. The fire hose was now hitting it full blast, but it seemed like a lost cause.

"You're gonna be okay." The paramedic patted me on the back. "Looks like luck was on your side."

"Definitely," I said.

He sighed. "Wrong answer." The paramedic morphed into Finch. "God was on your side. God, not luck. Have you learned nothing?"

"Finch!" I pulled the oxygen mask off. "Finally you show up! You missed everything. You should've seen what I did in there."

"You?" He arched a brow.

"Well, not *all* me, but, you know, God working through me. I should still get credit for the assist."

He smiled and nudged me. "You did great."

"Where were you?" I backhanded his shoulder. "I was praying like crazy. I needed you. I almost died up on that roof."

"I was there. Me and my crew. We brought the windstorm, Old Testament style."

"That was you? And ... other angels."

He nodded. "Pretty rad, huh? And what about you?" He gave me a playful punch. "You made me proud up there."

"Yeah, well, I thought I was dead. She had blackmail on me, she even threatened the lives of my friends."

"Lies and bluster." Finch waved off my worry. "That's a demon's bread and butter. Don't worry, nothing she threatened will come to pass. That security video of you at the dock is from a distant security cam on a foggy night. No positive ID's will come of it. Other than that, police testimony has multiple, conflicting descriptions of a Ms. Callow. One felon even claiming she's a witch. Couple that with claims about a drug-running kid named Harry that witnesses described as a grown up Harry Potter and the case is already a joke downtown. They've nicknamed it the Hogwarts drug ring. You're in the clear."

It was like a heavy weight lifting off my shoulders. "So, I'm free? She's got nothing on me?"

He nodded. "Fear is the enemy's primary weapon. They can't touch your spirit, so they bark as loud as they can."

I exhaled slowly, my muscles relaxing as the stress of the night fell away. "Still, I hope I never see her again."

"You won't," Finch said. "Her foothold here is broken. The tide has turned. She never saw it coming. Years of prayers and laboring of the saints is all coming to fruition, starting tonight."

"Really? But, the soup kitchen. I mean, it's lost. We don't have the money to fix it."

"I wouldn't worry about it." Finch gathered his paramedic equipment and stood. "Well, I'd better be off."

"Wait." I scrambled to my feet. "You're leaving?"

"They took me off probation." He smiled. "Looks like us teaming up together had some good results after all." Finch pointed upward. "He knows what He's doing."

"So ... that's it?" I said. "You're not gonna be around anymore?"

He shrugged. "You never know. For now, duty calls. Got a DH2 trying to start up a church in Vegas." Finch folded his hands. "God help me."

"But what if I need you?" I said. "What if things get all screwed up again?"

"Remember." He pointed up. "I'm just the messenger."

I stared at him a few moments. "I can't believe I'm saying this, but I'm actually gonna miss you."

Finch smiled and spread his arms out. "Come on, bring it in."

I gave him a big hug and felt my eyes tear up a bit.

He pulled back and pointed at me. "By the way, I'm recommending you for a TH level 3. I'm fairly certain of approval."

"TH?" I said. "As in Terrific Human?"

"Tolerable," Finch said.

I raised my eyebrows. "Are you kidding me? I just stopped a demon."

"You?"

"Again, I was a part of it."

"Don't worry. Once you hit level ten you transition to Pleasant Human." He flashed a thumbs up. "You're on your way."

Finch looked over his shoulder. Amber was heading our way in her green coupe.

"That's my cue." Finch put out his hand. "Pleasure working with you, Chris."

I grabbed his hand. "Likewise ... Godspeed Finchelus."

Finch winked and vanished in a twinkling of lights as Amber pulled up.

"Come on." Amber waved me over. "I've got great news."

I hopped into the car, and Amber headed down the street.

"I just got a call from Gwen." Amber's face lit up. "A donor just pledged all the money needed to save the soup kitchen."

"Serious?" A rush of excitement went through me. "Who?"

She met me with a wicked grin. "Like you don't know."

"I don't. Honest. Who is it?"

"Phillip Brantum," she said. "He said he met one of the Caring Table volunteers named Chris in a coffee shop this morning. It inspired him to donate. We don't have anyone else named Chris on our staff. It was you, right?"

"Well, yeah." I gave a slow nod, reeling from the news. "It was me but ... I mean, I had no idea he would donate anything. I only talked with the guy for a couple minutes about his nephew."

Amber shook her head. "Well, you must've said something right. When he found out the building was hit by vandals and burned, he promised to get things back up and running, whatever the cost." She grabbed my hand and squeezed firmly. "Chris, I can't tell you what this means to me. To a lot of people."

"Wow." I sat back, unable to speak for a few moments. "We did it. I mean, we actually did it."

There was such a joy flowing within me, I couldn't remember the last time, if ever, that I felt this fulfilled. I never imagined something that didn't have much to do with me or my personal goals would bring such meaning to my life.

Amber was all smiles. "You've really done something great, Chris."

I brought her hand to my lips. "You must be rubbing off on me."

She flashed a warm smile.

We turned a corner and the silhouette of palm trees against the backdrop of city lights spread across the windshield. A profound sense of me peace filled me. I exhaled deeply as we drove down the hill side, heading for home.

ACKNOWLEDGMENTS

I want to thank my wife and best friend Jolene for her support and priceless help brainstorming, reviewing rough drafts, copy editing, laughing at my jokes, and encouraging me every step of the way.

Special appreciation goes out to my amazing editor, Rebecca LuElla Miller, for her unmatched talent as a wordsmith. I am so grateful for her feedback and professional editing work on this novel.

A big thank you to Jenny Zemanek at Seedlings Design Studio for the fantastic cover art. Her work is incredible!

Lastly, I wanted to thank my critique group for their encouragement when I presented the first few chapters of my rough draft. They gave me the confidence I needed that I was on the right track. Thank you, Merrie, Becky, and Rachel!

All my love to Jolene, Joshua, and Katie.

Paul Regnier is a speculative fiction author perpetually lost in daydreams of spaceships, magic, and the supernatural. He is the writer of the Space Drifters series, a sci-fi/space opera comedy.

Paul is a technology junkie, drone pilot, photographer, web designer, drummer, Star Wars nerd, and a wannabe Narnian with a fascination for all things futuristic. Paul lives in Treasure Valley, Idaho, with his wife and two children.

Connect with Paul!

Website: www.PaulJRegnier.com

Newsletter sign-up:
https://landing.mailerlite.com/webforms/landing/x2v7m8
Facebook: www.Facebook.com/pjregnierauthor
Twitter: www.Twitter.com/PaulJRegnier
Instagram: www.Instagram.com/PaulJRegnier
Pinterest: www.Pinterest.com/PJRegnier

Made in the USA
Columbia, SC
27 June 2019